All

But

One

Collected Stories and a Novella

Reid Baron

All But One
Collected Stories and a Novella

Copyright © Reid Baron 2021

ISBN: 9798700747721

—

For Deb, Alexander and Oliver

Tell them to be patient

For they are all there

All but one, I, Chingachgook

The Last of the Mohicans

      James Fenimore Cooper/Michael Mann

Table of Contents

Short Stories

The General 7

The Incredible Hunk 21

The Dark Ages 37

Morning Coffee With a Political Junkie 45

Miss Hap Goes to Paris 59

Soccer Zombies Coming Soon 73

Frankenstein Meets the Behemoth,
or a Likely Story 85

Over Our Heads 97

Any News is Good 113

Novella

Witches' Coffee, 143
a Miracle Brew from Brazil

The General

1.

Someone must have planted those two royal palms, long ago, for nature never made such plans. Likewise the hill behind the general's ranch: the delicate tropical forest was gone, cleared away, and the naked red slope nurtured evergreen saplings where the jungle had once tenderly hung, like a Japanese screen.

General Vinicius's house had a corrugated iron roof for shucking off the interminable rains which accounted for the earth's habit of green. Banana leaves, sliced and shredded by the wind waved green translucent streamers, whenever the sun appeared. A snake, like a rigid length of rope, lay dead in the road, green. Every other hummingbird was luminous green. Only the general's iron roof and the naked slope in back of his ranch were red, the color of clay.

The old man always said he had a sweet tooth for the country. Nothing could spoil it -- these hills with their candied smell. Even now, when he'd arrive amidst a cortege of black sedans, surrounded by plain clothes men who sat in the cars, fondling big automatics that lay open to view on their laps he'd smile -- breathing in deep. A military man! And someday -- President?

From the road the general's garden, tucked between the red slopes at the back of his house, couldn't be seen. The old man spent hours there, absorbed in his thoughts and gardening. Silently, he worked with a farmhand, a local man, who'd never eaten a thing he hadn't raised with his own two hands. Inside a chain link enclosure out front by the road, where the general wouldn't be disturbed by seeing them, sullen bodyguards in purple shirts circled, nervously.

Atop the sunbaked hill, a sharpshooter would be hidden in the remaining jungle. Higher still, falcons drifted and wheeled. Smaller birds darted in crisscrossing curves, running for bugs. Butterflies made wavering pastel targets. The general, in a green boiler man's suit, pottered around his garden with the local man.

2.

In his garden the general tended a rank of lettuce, taking the grey watering can from his helper, Eduardo. "Blast those loudspeakers," he said. "Spoiling my weekend."

It was election year. Small cars with electric megaphones on top penetrated each and every recess of the nation, blaring out familiar political rosters with unending strings of achievements. Forbidden the mention of objectives, blurred to static by improper wiring, the messages were a barely comprehensible nuisance.

Eduardo said, "May I ask--when are the elections, General?"

"Next week," said the old man. "You must be sure to vote."

"Will your name be there?"

"No, no..." the general laughed, looking up from the feet of one cabbage row. "But you can vote for da Silva, from my party."

"What would he do?" The farmhand crushed a leaf-eating sauva ant under a black boot toe.

—

General Vinicius straightened to full stature, white-haired against the red slope in his green gardener's suit. "The government develops the country," he said. "And rids us of obstacles, like the subversives."

"Any of these subversives around here?"

"I don't think so."

"Patron, if I saw one, how would I know?"

"It'd be easy to tell...they don't act like regular men."

"Why, what do they do?"

The general thought for a moment. "Well, if a man came along and pulled you out of your house -- left you standing in the cold while he took everything you owned -- then burned your house down, that would be a subversive.

"Hmmn." Eduardo grunted. Bending down, he said, "Should we dig up a few of these turnip seedlings and put them here?"

The general nodded yes, fine, the turnips'll be fine there. It doesn't much matter that I gave no order -- this country man knows his plants. He's been living at this crossroad now for fifty years. Before, way before we grew sugar cane for Arabian kings...but anyway, it's the weekend, and the party in power, my party, always wins.

3.

Slouched against the bunkhouse wall near the far corner of the chain link enclosure on that sunny Saturday morning Sgt. Geraldo of the special detail was reading a newspaper. He had a full view of the road from where he sat, for the grass was cut short: it was a flat, highly controllable space. Geraldo read. Prices would go up; potatoes would not be available for three months; his favorite soccer star Hilario had been sold to a rival club, Santos. In a suburban district, police had executed a cocaine dealer. Who were the officers? Him? That cross-eyed jerk? He couldn't even shoot straight.

The locals bounced back and forth along the read in their donkey carts while Geraldo sat in the sun, reading. Not much action to be sure, but the general's gate was a stopping place for the old plantation bus, and you had to watch when the crowds gathered there, four times a day. Really nothing to do -- keep one eye on the road, watch for new faces, read the paper, try to spend most of the time in the shade, think ahead.

A brown and white paint pony, the finest horse in the neighborhood, danced up and down the road all that morning, while Geraldo read. Riderless, it went crashing off into the brush to feed, scooping its head and tossing its mane. Geraldo watched it circle; saw it break into a youthful trot when two black dogs chased. Wouldn't it be fine to own one of those? Someone was calling him from a corner of the fence.

Snapping out of his distraction, Geraldo shot up straight.

"Hello there, good afternoon." An old man leaned on a staff opposite the bunkhouse, outside the fence. A green hill hovered in sunlight behind his head.

"Aha old fellow, what do you say?"

"Everything OK?"

"One hundred per cent."

—

"And what about the old Englishman?...He used to pay me ten..."

The ancient figure took two steps down the road that led past the bunkhouse in the direction of the general's ranch. The sun appeared behind his head.

"I don't know him -- what are you talking about?"

The old man stopped, supporting himself on his staff. "Ten, ten every time he came!"

Sgt. Geraldo threw down his paper. He had never seen this old man before. "Hold on," he shouted. "Where are you trying to get to in that direction?"

"You mean the old boy isn't around: the one who used to pay?"

Geraldo put his hand on his hip, and took one step toward an alarm buzzer fixed by the side of the bunkhouse door. Behind him, the black sedans drank in the sun and shone, sated with it. Rays poured in through the bullet-proof windows, yellowing day-old newspapers that sat on the seats. Geraldo tensed.

A small boy raced by, rolling a bicycle rim with a thin switch. The brown and white pony came crashing out of the bush again.

Why don't I fire into the air over this old man's head -- Geraldo grimaced --if he takes another step? He felt for his holster, loosened the snap, and tasted adrenalin.

"Oh, what a shame -- then the old boy's gone, I have to go away." Turning, the old man leaned on his staff and headed back in the direction from which he had come.

4.

If there's a turncoat in the group I'll know it, General Vinicius was thinking. They were stopped that morning across from the gazebo in the nearby town: his wife had suggested that they shop for dry goods. The general followed her into the store, relaxed enough in beige casual trousers and a yellow summer-weight shirt. Two black cars stuck close to the curb, a sun-suited, sun-glassed special detail inside plastered against grey tinted windows: alert, pistol hands at their hips. I've been warned, the general thought, handling a small planter's shovel. Did he have one like it already?

His intelligence advisers supposed there were subversives in another small village twenty minutes down the road, though what those pests might be accomplishing in that placid town, the general couldn't imagine.

Most of their kind had been driven out of the papers and into the jungle years before; far enough from the halls of order and justice, and the corridors of progress. The general rotated a can of insecticide, studying the label's tactics.

Better to fight poison with poison, he thought as the cashier made change; as far as the country was concerned, subversives were no different than leaf-cutting ants.

Walking back to his sedan with the pesticide wrapped in a brown bag, the general smiled at these orderly connections: he could have them written into his next speech. Ah, there was the trouble -- a security man shielded the general's body as he joined his wife in the car – these

—

people from the city. If someone tries to do me in, it'll be one of these, a friend, a disciplined military man, frustrated by the slow development of his career.

Satisfied, the general reviewed the week's events with his wife.

The dark caravan rode the last few miles from town to his ranch. When the cars left asphalt to travel over dirt everyone widened their eyes, taking in the prettified former plantation. Over the green forested hills black magpies gathered, then floated down one-by-one on glider wings.

The general's face, framed in a rear window, bore a look that was composed, serene.

5.

By ten a.m. the next morning Eduardo had not shown up for work. The general stood, green-suited and ready to garden, between the ranch house with its red iron roof and the clay-toned hillside slope, towering above his cherished plants, hands wrapped around a rake. He heard the paint pony's hooves tapping out front in the road, above that rhythm some ancient disconnected singsong floated. Now-- where was that brilliant gardener?

Above the birds chirped, climbing and diving in formation, wing-to-wing. Bugs scraped out a serenade of messages in their electronic code -- intended war? Yes! The general saw trains of ants stagger through his planted hillocks, struggling under scissored burdens. Where's that lazy guy, he thought; I'll need something to keep these magpies out of my cabbage. Something.

Out of earshot when the maid called everyone to lunch, the general had disappeared within his garden shed.

Absorbed, be searched among the hanging hoes and rakes, gathering odd sticks and poles, rags and twine and straw. He rifled through a box of old fabrics. On the porch, the maid gave up calling and walked back to the kitchen. The general checked his watch, and when he saw he'd missed a meal, laughed, and went on with his project in the shed. He was startled when Geraldo's shadow blocked the sunlight from the door.

"What!" he jumped. "Why aren't you eating with the rest?"

Sgt. Geraldo fought to demonstrate seriousness and control. "General, I'm off duty until four."

"Good..." The old man let pieces fall to camouflage his task and free his hands. Sensing more, be snapped, "Then what are you doing in here? Why did you leave your post?"

Sgt. Geraldo brought his hand with the newspaper up to swat a fly, and lost his nerve when he saw how the general froze. "I just wanted to know," he shifted gears, "if you've ever seen a crazy man with a staff walking around here, talking to himself?"

General Vinicius muttered words under his breath to demonstrate rank, betray no loss of composure. He took a few brisk steps past Sgt. Geraldo and continued the conversation from outside the damp shed. Standing in the warm sunlight, he began, "Yes, I've seen him."

"What are your orders, sir?"

"What of it? A lunatic, a crazy old man. There are plenty, hereabouts, where we can't provide any care," the general gritted his teeth.

—

Geraldo frowned. "I'll scare him off then, next time he comes around...fire a shot over his head..."

The general looked into Sgt. Geraldo's face, "No, it's no use...Don't bother."

"Well, Then I see: he's no trouble." Geraldo said. "He goes on about something that must have happened twenty years ago..."

Staring fixedly through the garden rows to the half-naked slope, the general changed the subject. "Have you seen Eduardo?" he asked.

"No, General Vinicius. He's probably lying on the floor of his shack half-drunk..."

"And he's the best of these country folk," the general scowled, not amused. "This damned Brazil! Drunk, insane or dumb." He looked back in Geraldo's direction.

Geraldo walked quickly past the general, saluting with total respect.

He said, "I guess I'd better return to my post." |

"Fine," the general said, returning a semi-salute. He went into the shed and picked up the pieces of his project, trying new angles, tying and fiddling around, twisting threads.

6.

At the window, the general watched the setting sun shimmer over the garden, sending rosy skeins through the sky and burnishing the image of his wife, seated at the dining table, with the fireplace crackling in the warm room. Open before her was a copy of the day's paper. Turning from the window to find her there, the general remembered his wife's body as it had once been, the valleys and hills, like the hills that stood between him and town, exactly what it had taken to get to where he was. Maneuvers and turns, valleys and hills.

"Somebody's been trying to do me in," the general said to his wife.

"Vinicius, you shouldn't be telling me things like that if you don't mean them." The old lady scarcely looked up from her paper. "You know they frighten me."

Staring past her at the antique spinning wheel they'd bought at an auction, and at the rest of the room -- the fireplace, wall hangings, green love seats and sofas, a large wedding painting they had commissioned during another age – the general said nothing.

"It's not like the old days," his wife said. "Things like that never happen anymore."

The general turned from her to gaze once again through the window to the garden. A dusky mist had settled among the sown ranks, like the vapor of memory layering phases of life past.

"But it's true," he said. "I know 1 shouldn't talk too freely, but I can feel it, around us, closing in."

"Enough of that nervous chatter, General Vinicius Correia!" His wife was buried in her newspaper. "If there's any trouble you have six security men here. And the plantation's only phone."

'What do you know?' the general thought. He looked into his wife's face, and saw it as it had been, the face of a priceless Rio nymph stretched out on a lounge beside her father's swimming pool. He said, "It could be one of those men..."

"What...Ay! Look here!" Sra. Fontes de Correia was pointing to the paper.

"Now what is it?"

"Look here in the paper: Something about a bishop – they beat him up and painted him red. How awful."

"I heard about that," said the general. "He was a subversive!"

The general's wife studied the photograph more carefully. Scenes played backward in recollection, and she said with regret, "It's terrible. Do you know who this is? This poor bishop was the priest who married us, thirty-six years ago..."

Back at the window, General Vinicius said, "So terrible things still happen, do they? But here's something good." He peered out through the screen. A cloud drifting over the jungle hill stole the last light from the garden. "Tomorrow we'll have rain," he said.

7.

Dusk came, shrouding the hills. Out came clouds of fireflies, mating in rituals that made brilliant constellations. A grey, serpentine iguana, streaks of yellow scaling it to prehistoric times, flashed out of its shelter beneath the general's agave plant, distrustful, alert. Dogs barked at anything.

From the nearby village a panel truck crept out onto the highway, carrying a group of men and women. Leaflets spilled out of brown cartons that squashed when they sat. Not a word was spoken. They drove through the oncoming night, feeling the mountainous dips of the road that led toward the ranch with queasy stomachs.

Sgt. Geraldo sat in the bunkhouse fiddling with his automatic. With a decisive motion, he got up off his bed. He crept out the door, through the gate in the chain link fence, and onto the darkening fragrant road. The hills were black smudges in the evening's ink. Geraldo searched the skyline where it met hilltop behind the general's garden. He remembered he'd seen the marksman's feet protruding from his narrow bed in the bunkhouse; the man was asleep. He'd better get on with it then.

Now the panel truck slowed and bumped over ruts the rains had endlessly grooved into the clay plantation road. Tangled forests clung to the dark, sloping hillsides. Stopping by a stately mango tree in a square surrounded by shadowy huts, the riders dropped softly from the truck and

fanned out in the direction of the general's ranch. A mule hoarsely brayed.

Mists drifted down the jungle hillsides; frogs croaked a punctuation for the evening from the bottomlands edging the streams. Underground springs fed these waters that, coursing steadily through the darkness, were the pulse of the land. The half-dozen figures circling the general's garden felt the rush of their blood drown out the streams' soothing, continuous hum.

Sgt. Geraldo, crouched near the shed, saw the subversives take up positions at the corners of the garden fence. And he was sure he saw the crazy old man heading

—

toward his general in the center of the garden. It may be that to save his skin, he started the shooting then, by firing into the air. Or perhaps he fired with the subversives, a torrent of bullets that riddled two figures in the garden, the curious and crazy old man, and the dutiful scarecrow.

Full of holes, the scarecrow would be seen the next day, standing over the body of the lunatic (once a state governor somebody claimed) where the general had resolutely hung it, in the center of the garden, smartly dressed in medals and an officer's hat, in military green.

The Incredible Hunk

"Here we are, mon."

The nation was poised that Saturday afternoon, waiting for the match-up between Billy Botchko and the Incredible Hunk. This was for the Zenith Universal Association title in wrestling, and nobody wanted to miss it.

I was at ringside talking to Purple Man, the Rastafarian wrestler who had got to be the Hunk's best pal. You know: he's the guy who perfected the Painless Death Hold—he comes out and makes a peace speech before the match, instead of talking tough. The trouble is, you have to be sure to call him 'Purple Mon', or there's no kind of cooperation you can expect.

I don't mind—you might as well be a Rastafarian these days as anything, if you want to have religion: none of the others really seems to work. But I was never much for religion.

The Rastafarian was giving me some details of his friend the Hunk's past history, things most people would like to know about....

"Yah, mon," he was saying, "you know everybody tinks all dis such a big joke. The Hunk, he such a sweetheart of every gal. And how's this big, beautiful playboy swan fight for real and troo? But nobody know how he was before, when he got cut so bad..."

My mouth was watering for that info, you can bet. What people do know about, what they have seen plenty of, is the Hunk's magnificent torso, alongside a procession of starlets and models—sometimes more than one at a time. Out on the town in his bulging tux, his stylish blond locks and cool blue eyes captured during an intimate moment of ultimate socializing harmony, in Bachelor Heaven on the cover of a magazine. And the women all saying he's really charming, the gentlest of men. Could there really be a sordid story, something ugly wrapped up, well-hidden and just about forgotten inside that prize-package fortress of strength. I was shaking my head.

"Yah, mon, Purple Mon is telling you troo. Dere's not too many who knows about it, for sure. He were a different mon."

"Would the Hunk want you to say?"

"We are brothers, mon, no problem. Everything with the Hunk and Purple Mon be totally coool. I and I am soon to educate you on what really went down."

"Ok, Purple Mon," I told him. "But why pick me?"

"Mon, have you got not fee-it (that's how he says faith)? I mon am telling you it's all right, mon, coool. Cause I know how de Incredible Hunk tink. He trust you, he tink you are a Mon of Troot. We learned to read with you stories in Wrestlemania Times."

"Thanks, Purple Mon, I never heard about that."

With the match coming on in less than an hour and tension and strain building in the gym, I couldn't help but think this particular truth might turn out to be dangerous. But how could you say that to a Righteous Rasta who had taken the wrestling world by surprise, threatening if necessary to 'kill so easy de other mon feel no pee-en (pain)?'

—

Who very likely would be pitting his Painless Death Hold against his handsome brother in de ring, one of his Soon-Coming days. These were men whose boasts were big enough to dare you to doubt them by no means.

"You're telling me the Hunk wasn't always so pretty?"

"Yes, mon, it's for sure true. When he comin up he was handsome, and always work long hours, building in de gym. And the gals like him too, but not so much as now."

"What happened, Purple Mon?"

"Yah, man, it was in the Philly Spectrum. He go inna tag team match with Angel John McKnight and mon, he get cut with a razor by the Rattlesnake Kid. Slit him from ear to Adam's apple."

"Goodness," I said. "When was this, Purple Mon? I never heard that story about the Hunk."

"Yah mon, that's what you go to know. This wrestler who get cut in Philly—you probably don't remember him. He called Swedish Son Johnson then and dropped out of wrestling after the tragic incident."

"The Swedish Son," I said, thinking it over. "There's not many who recall such a fleeting figure on the scene."

"Sure mon. But how about de Alien Exterminator? The man who never reveal de identity behind he mask...?"

"Right! And after he won the Association title he never wrestled again. Just vanished into thin air. Why, he never even went to pick up the title belt."

Purple Man's story suddenly made sense to me, along with the startling revelation that our gorgeous Incredible Hunk had hidden his tarnished looks for years behind a mask, acting out all that terrible destruction we had thought of as the trademark of the Alien Exterminator, a deadly and mysterious figure who gave no quarter and inflicted unnecessary pain. Meanwhile, a plastic surgeon slowly must have returned his youthful ruggedness to the Swede, who popped out of the cocoon to become our much beloved champ, The Incredible Hunk. It made me look forward to the afternoon's title defense match with a new sense of anticipation, and more than a little bit of fear. Emerging from my trance, I looked up at Purple Man.

"Yah, mon," he said, in his comprehending way. "You are seeing it all. Meditate it well, now, Mon of Troot."

Yes, indeed. What would happen, I wondered, contemplating the excesses of the challenger, Billy Botchko, aka The Executioner, The Quasher, The Polish Renegade...an embittered defector from Eastern Europe whose view of life was so negative that he refused to apply for citizenship in the nation that took him in and made him a wealthy wrestler. A man with no country or creed, devoted solely to brutality and mayhem. Could the Incredible Hunk survive their bout intact, with all of his re-constituted good looks? Now it suddenly seemed to represent a terrific struggle not simply to determine whether good and beauty could defeat hideous ugliness and evil, but whether that entire process was forever doomed to regression, a circle with no progress.

Purple Man, already a head taller than me, was now looking to be further and further away. He seemed to behold me from a great distance, regarding me from within his tangle of locks, far, far away.

—

"Yah, mon," he said to me. "You are feelin' it deep. You know it all the way down to de roots. Meditate it and realize it well, mon. Edjicate yisself, breathe it in."

"What's going to happen, Purple Mon?" Panicky, I felt like rushing into the ring and begging Vic Allison not to announce the contenders, not to let the match begin. Then I thought I would dash over to the TV crew and tell them it was too horrible a thing for anybody to see...as if they would care.

Just then the harsh, keening sound of Billy Botchko's theme music was heard. There was a great stirring of anticipation in the arena: the contestants would soon be making their way down to the squared circle, the combat zone, the place of truth.

"We are here, mon," Purple Man's voice came to me out of ringside cigar smoke mists. "Be cool, mon. Soon come Billy Botchko, and the Incredible Hunk also come soon, and we are close by, mon, you and me, very near, very close to it—We mon in the presence of the Inside and Inner and Almighty Troot. We are here mon, just you watch an wee-it."

Suddenly there was a cascade of female screams. But these were not the screams of love like you heard for the Beatles, not yet. It was Billy Botchko coming out, and the ladies were filled with fear, afraid for the mutilation of their charming, corporeal heartthrob: The Incredible Hunk.

Botchko was a kind of exquisitely dressed fat slob. That is, he came out in a tall top hat and tails, a tight garment he would gradually strip to reveal an executioner's leather pants and vest. But then you saw that he was a butcher; his body was not as shapely as it had looked, restrained inside the tux—he was a murderous, brutish hog. Accompanying Botchko's awful clashing music, tides of fan feeling swept the arena, set in motion by the monstrous wrestler and his retinue of thugs surging down the aisle thru the crowd.

"See him, Mon of Troot? Him too much fatness!"

"Yes, Purple Mon." I had never like Billy Botchko, but that's another story.

Botchko climbed through the ropes and strode around the ring, taking vicious swipes at the air with his plastic axe. He handed the prop to his manager and commenced to strip down, peeling off the wrapping of civilization to reveal his foreign mass of blubber. Meanwhile, the top hat remained, making you fear all the more, as if there was some minimal, cool, killer's pro calculation driving this primal blob to incorporate anything it could.

"He so ugly," said Purple Man. "Even I and I am full with de feeling of fee-er."

Now the crowd began to settle and quiet down, exhausted by trading insults with Billy Botchko's crew, and riding the tides of hatred Botchko had brought with him into the arena. A sense of expectation, of hopefulness, was unfolding in that moment of calm.

The Incredible Hunk's theme music began to play over the loudspeakers then. It was the ballad Some Enchanted Evening, sung by the Italian Enzio Pinza on the original Broadway recording of South Pacific. An old and scratchy 78 rpm copy of the album was always used, for it

—

gave added poignancy to this romantic number, which seemed to tell of the different passions of a bygone age…

'Some enchanted evening

You may see a stranger

You may see a stranger

Across a crowded room…'

In the corner of the arena nearest the dressing rooms, the strange things that happened every time the Hunk came out were starting to occur. Female fans had developed the habit of putting locks of their hair, telephone numbers and other tokens of their love into plastic bags, which they would shower upon the Hunk as he moved down the aisle toward the ring. Currently the grandstand was pouring down this plastic rain. And there came the wailing-moans, a special sort of sound nobody had ever heard before, but which by now, everyone knew. Then the actual motion of the champ and his bodyguards toward the ring started snaking waves throughout the crowd.

"Here he comes," I said to Purple Man.

"De time is nee-er."

The Incredible Hunk's staff had arranged for the tailoring of special finery for his title defense, basically a souped-up version of his regulation costume. It was the white suit of a Renaissance swashbuckler, a Romeo out of Romeo and Juliet, and his white hat was crested with feathery egret plumes. Decorating the white silk suit and cape in strategic locations was a pattern of padded and quilted red hearts. There were big red hearts tattooed on the Hunk's well-developed biceps and one stood out on his chest. Under his arm he always carried an oversized address book with a heart on its cover, and this he would kiss and hold high above his head as he made his way down to the ring.

"Can you see him, Purple Mon?" Cigar smoke and moans were choking the arena, and the Rastafarian had to stand on tiptoes, even at six-foot-six.

"Ya mon—look at he. He so elegant coool."

"I hope he'll win, Purple Mon."

Purple Man looked, now serenely, up at Billy Botchko, who stomped the ring like a vicious and impatient bull. He had never been matched against the Polish Renegade himself.

"Soon come de moment, Mon of Troot," he said wistfully to me. "Soon come. I and I and everybody soon to know."

Plastic bags full of blonde and raven and red and auburn tresses were landing around our feet. The Incredible Hunk mounted the steps to the ring. He put down his address book and threw his plumed hat out to the ringside seats, creating a frenzy of scrambling gals. He hung his cape neatly over the ropes and stripped off his tunic with its pattern of bright red hearts. He got down to his wrestling shorts, which had small hearts embroidered at the hip sockets—meanwhile the wailing-moans chorused on. The theme music was shut off and Vic Allison stepped up to the hanging mike to announce the title match.

Billy Botchko snarled like a rabid dog and his top hat waggled atop his head while the ring announcer spoke. Meanwhile, the Incredible Hunk travelled around the ring, waving over the ropes to the crowd. Women in the areas where he directed his glances went into panic motions. He spotted me and Purple Man at ringside and raised a clenched fist.

"Coool."

The match for the Zenith Universal Association heavyweight title in wrestling was about to begin. Billy Botchko kept stomping around in the center of the ring, his executioner's eyes bullets in a fat face, his leather pants going ram-rod stiff in support of almost 400 pounds of bulky mass. His tall hat ticked like the second hand of a countdown timepiece. He stared straight into the back of the Incredible Hunk's head, while the champ kept waving to the crowd.

And then there was a great, fearful roar.

"He rushin' im before he ready!"

Sure enough, Billy Botchko slammed into the Hunk's back, bending him over the top rope, yelling to the crowd, "Take one last look at this handsome face."

And what could you read in that countenance?

In the depths of those ultramarine blue eyes was there a sleepy satisfaction, sense of noble purpose, or the cold concentration of a man trying to bear intense pain? And what about the curly blonde hair, the pink cheeks that had been repaired, and were now so smooth and flawless and serene? Was it all effortless? Or did the sad memory leave its mark? Only now there was a red flush in the Incredible Hunk's face, as he strained to get the monster Botchko off his back and resume the match on equal terms.

And he did! Applying his famous Five Finger Grip to Billy Botchko's hands, the Hunk managed to escape the full nelson that had him had him bent forward over the ropes. Then he did something that justified his gymnastic reputation: holding onto the top rope where he'd been pinned, he swung down onto the arena floor, and vaulted back up again, flying over Billy Botchko's head. He wound up standing in the center of the ring, grinning at the enraged Botchko.

"Did you see that?" I said to Purple Man.

"Him is the only one as can do it in de whole whirl…Dem is two top rankin', for sure, Mon of Troot."

The Hunk then strode forward toward the snarling Botchko, and they traded tremendous karate chops and tested one another's strength by handgrips for nearly a full minute. No real progress was being made, and then suddenly, Botchko swung the Hunk into the ropes and prepared to lay a massive body slam on him. But the champ leapt right over him and from behind, chopped Botchko squarely between the shoulder blades. The massive and blubbery body quivered and shook with the force of the blow, but like a wounded rhino Billy Botchko came forward, not really hurt, just seeing red and ready to do some heavy harm.

Billy Botchko lifted his leather-covered right leg twice, with surprising agility, and kicked the Hunk squarely in the chest. The Hunk reeled backward onto the ropes and prepared to field the Polish Renegade's insane charge. Just as Botchko reached him, the Hunk deftly sidestepped the attack, and sliding one hand along the top rope to steady himself, jumped up into the air and kicked Billy Botchko's top hat right off of his head. It tumbled into the crowd.

—

A fearsome wailing-moan issued from the women's throats. While its echo haunted the arena, the Hunk's supporters urged him to take advantage of the disoriented Billy Botchko.

But along with his top hat, the Renegade had lost his last shred of refinement. He simply went wild. He rushed forward, slamming his head into the Hunk's midsection, driving the champ onto the ropes. There the Incredible Hunk remained, seemingly stunned, while Billy Botchko rammed his brainless cranium into the champ's mid-section again and again.

How long could the Hunk handle the assaults of the 400-pound, sub-human battering ram? Would his rib cage merely cave in? Or would Billy Botchko work on weakening the Incredible Hunk just enough so that he could introduce one of his beloved foreign objects, like a rusty nail or a screwdriver, and make good his pre-match boast to "Mess up duh pretty boy's face"?

"I and I am feelin de fee-er down deep, Mon of Troot," said Purple Man. "I tink the Hunk can't deny Billy Botchko he hate-ful vi-er-lence…He gwan make de champ pay!"

Sure enough, Billy Botchko began waving one hand in the air, gloating in triumph each time he rammed into the dazed Incredible Hunk. Anyone who knew about this vicious monster and his hideous ways was aware that this was the fatal sign of the moment when Botchko would produce a pointed item from some hidden pocket and prepare to mutilate another wrestler who had been, 'stupid enough to fight fair.'

"No, no, no!" came the shouts of the crowd, soaring above the persistent wailing-moans. It was a hideous and fearsome symphony to hear.

Billy Botchko stood in the center of the ring, laughing like a madman who has just landed on his feet outside the asylum wall. He was lookin down at his right hand, where a beer can opener has appeared, and he was laughing like a hyena. The Incredible Hunk saw it and rushed him, trying to kick the sharp object away, but Billy Botchko held on, grazing the Hunk's shin in the process. There was a tiny trickle of blood.

Intimidated by Botchko's boast that he would kill everyone if he had a chance, the referee was spending his time cowering in the corner of the ring. But then something peculiar happened—a woman had left her seat, somehow evaded security and was climbing into the ring, holding onto the bottom rope.

The Hunk saw her first, and an expression of horror crossed his face, twisting the resolve he had been mustering to overcome his disadvantage and defeat Botchko into an expression of momentary worry and confusion. He tried to motion the woman back, but as he did so, Billy Botchko crashed an immense forearm behind his ear, driving the Hunk to the mat. He lay there for an instant, stunned.

Meanwhile, the woman had come to her feet at the other side of the ring. Half the crowd was moaning in fear for the Hunk, others were pleading for the woman to get out of the ring, a third contingent was urging her on to somehow get in Billy Botchko's way and help the Incredible Hunk. Screams and moans and shouts collided in the arena and pandemonium reigned.

—

Billy Botchko stood, glaring down at the Hunk, savoring the prospect of the champ's total destruction. As far as the championship belt was concerned, you had to wonder whether the Polish Renegade even cared what that was about. Carnage was the only notion ruffling the smooth surface of his pea brain.

The woman did not look to be any kind of female wrestler. She was thin, with dirty blonde hair, and wore jeans and an Incredible Hunk tee-shirt, the one where an arrow goes thru a broken heart on the back, and which says, simply 'I Love You Incredible Hunk' on the front. As she crept tentatively across the ring behind Billy Botchko's back you could see tears trickling down the lady's cheeks, and a look of determination, of one offended, struggling to overcome the downright sadness of her beautiful brown eyes. Perhaps this woman who had thrown a plastic bag at other of the Hunk's matches, and waited and hoped, but whether or not he had ever called her number, she was there now, creeping up behind the monster Botchko, with a likely foredoomed idea in mind.

While the crowd begged, wept, moaned or yelled for blood Botchko hesitated, waiting to deliver a crushing body blow that would paralyze the Hunk. After that, Botchko would get to work with his can opener, returning the Incredible Hunk to a condition of hideous savagery equal to his own.

The woman was right behind Botchko now, but he didn't sense it.

"Purple Mon, I can't look!"

"Do not turn away, Mon of Troot, ree-alize and consider well what happenin'."

Botchko was ready to drop when the frail blonde crept around him and knelt between him and the Incredible Hunk. She seemed to gain something from the nearness to the object of her affection and rather than supplicating, she shook a tiny, bloodless, bony fist in Billy Botchko's ugly face.

"Dare is a woman of strent," said Purple Man.

Billy Botchko's bullet eyes seemed to pop out of his head. But he did not laugh. Swiping with his left arm in one swift and powerful motion, he grabbed the woman's upraised fist and threw her fourteen rows back into the seats.

The crowd screamed. But the delay had given the Incredible Hunk enough time to roll clear of Billy Botchko, and to get to his feet across the ring. He called out to the crowd that he wouldn't forget what the woman had done. Then he steadied himself and prepared to launch his patented Fair Air Leap at Botchko, hoping to bring the big man down in a fall, to be injured by his own outsized mass. His blue eyes held a look of revenge for the insult and injury committed upon himself—and the woman who had bravely entered the ring to help him—his soft eyes blue eyes now gave off a diamond pure glow.

Whipping himself into the opposite ropes for added momentum the Incredible Hunk leapt. He flew across the empty space at the center of the ring like a missile in a Holy War. On the fly, he hit Botchko at his bulging beltline and dropped down in a heap, tangled with the monster, lost beneath elephantine flab. He did not move.

Billy Botchko stirred, awakening first from the collision. He rolled over halfway and found the Incredible

Hunk lying motionless beneath him like a piece of the mat. He took his can opener and began to rip the embroidered hearts away from the Hunk's wrestling briefs, shredding the silk outfit. He tore out the pieces and stood up to grind them demonically beneath his big boot. Then he bent down again, ready to begin cutting into the Hunk's face, good for his terrible word.

Right then I felt Purple Man emit a new vibration. He seemed to grow taller, but I was mistaken. He was climbing into the ring.

"Sometime need a posse," he said to me as he went up over the bottom rope. "Dis Billy Botchko, he no am a conscious yoot."

Purple Man, multitude of locks flying, crossed the ring with two swift steps. He rammed Billy Botchko at his hip socket as the monster was bent over, preparing to do his dirty work. Botchko fell to the mat with a terrible thud and, cursing, rolled over twice across the ring.

"Wash he mout out will we," Purple Man yelled to the fans.

They were on their feet. Reggae music began to pound out, and everyone was dancing. It was Dennis Brown singing:

Time to separate the sheep

From the wolves

We're at the crossroads

And this is the time of decision

The crowd rocked and swayed, standing on their seats. Billy Botchko was blindly searching around for his can opener, which he'd lost in tumbling to the mat.

Across the ring Purple Man stood waiting, and I thought I saw him wink.

Whether it was for real or not, well, make your own choice. In his struggle with Billy Botchko, what will happen to Purple Man—is he also wearing his heart on his briefs?

The Dark Ages

Juan Carlos and Marciano sat on the dusty step of a shop entryway in San Cristobal de las Casas, in the state of Chiapas, Mexico. Juan Carlos wore dark green pants and a beige short-sleeved cotton shirt, with corn stalks patterned lightly on the breast pockets. Over his solid blue shirt Marciano had on a cloud-grey wool serape to protect him, for he would walk for an hour back up the mountain to his home during a chilly afternoon. On his head sat a beat-up straw hat. The hat brim bent one way and the other in the lunch hour sunlight as Marciano watched Juan Carlos demonstrate the record player.

"I tell you 'mano, this record player is magic," said Juan Carlos. "I bought it from the gringo myself. The guy was out of money--broke--he had to sell!" Juan Carlos spoke quickly.

"And just what is magic about it?" asked the native Mexican, Marciano.

"Listen...you'll have nothing but good times with it, 'mano," continued Juan Carlos. "Because I'm selling it to you along with these four hit records. All number ones ! But, once you're tired of them, you'll see that you can get music directly from the turntable...Let me tell you, it's a real miracle."

"Let's see," Marciano said.

Juan Carlos held out the four pressed wafers: Downtown, by Petulia Clark; two long-plays: Roberto Carlos Canta Espanol and Los Dinner in Concert; along with another forty-five: Incense and Peppermint by the Strawberry Alarm Clock.

"It's not possible to show you that feature now," he said, "No... like I said, you have to be really tired of these four hit records first. And that takes time. Then the player will work with new records you buy or--like I'm telling you--by magic. Just put the needle right here on the rubber..."

The miraculous record-player, speaker and all, was no more than five inches high. As it ran on batteries as well as electric juice, Juan Carlos could show Marciano how to place the diamond stylus neatly onto the rotating flatbed without the presence of a record, holding the player-arm between a tendentious thumb and forefinger. Blap! Bad Sound! Immediately Juan Carlos picked the needle up from the turntable, not wanting to ruin the machine in advance of its magic moment. "See?"

Now Marciano was a penny-wise Native Mexican and nobody's fool. He had learned to distrust ladinos, as his people called their incompletely Indian Mexican brothers, for the arrangements of the ladino with the Natives were seldom equitable. But Marciano had serious intentions for the record player that possibly clouded his judgment.

In his village a man was elected every few months to finance the religious obligations of the group. You faced up to ruin in order to purchase a stock of skinny candles, some bright ribbons and streamers, to promote fireworks, hire a band and pay the priest. It was a test which, when the Indian man passed it, would add greatly to his prestige, making him a full-fledged member of his village community. Looking at the magic record player, Marciano saw smiles breaking across the seamed and implacable coppery faces of his village's ancient women as they heard it play a song of devotion at the next fiesta; he could hear the respectful compliments of his village brothers. The emotion that swelled in his breast in anticipation could not have been egotistical.

It was a matter of solemn duty that Marciano had sworn to in the village hall, accepting an obligation some men had been known to run from. But he was short on funds with which to purchase holy music. He bought the record player, after attempting to bargain down by eliminating the four hit records from the deal.

"Impossible," said Juan Carlos, accepting in trade ten embroidered blouses which Marciano's wife and her sisters had laboriously created, using miles of red and yellow thread they dyed in boiling kettles themselves. Each blouse had taken the family women two weeks to complete.

"And-don't- forget," said Juan Carlos, "the magic player won't work until you're good and tired of those four hit records and have no money to buy any others."

"You didn't tell me that before," said Marciano without blinking.

"Well, that's the way it is."

Stepping into the broken-cobbled, dusty street, Juan Carlos contemplated the lovely bundle of shirts he would shortly sell to a shop catering to tourists.

Marciano gathered up his burden, glanced once at the heavens, and wondered how he would get his things home dry considering the impending afternoon rainfall. Would he be able to make good on his promise to provide music for the festival, or be accounted a weak, deficient man ?

Quickly, Marciano jumbled the record player and four selections of pressed hot wax into his burlap sack. He began to trudge out of town toward the road that would take him toward his village, an hour and forty-five minute walk up stony paths, and more. He climbed up, into the wispy fog and drizzle, up slippery tracks etched into the forbidding grey-green cliffs, in the direction of the dark ages, some might say. The fog thickened, covering the Native who scrambled with small, rapid steps up the difficult hillside with a dank mist.

Sadly, within a month Marciano found himself in disgrace with the people of his small village. It wasn't that the magic player wouldn't work as such, no; the trouble was that with the fiesta coming up, Marciano was spending day and night listening to the four hit records, trying to tire himself of them. First it was Incense and Peppermint that made him sick; but long before that, his wife had begged him to take a walk down by the icy stream that skirted the village if he wanted to play with his miracle machine.

Next out of fashion with Marciano were the raucous top-forty instrumentals of Los Dinner--a 70's Mexican show band who always played their dates in white tuxedos. Petulia Clark's brash and brassy Downtown tired Marciano a little later. Last went the translations into Spanish of the Brazilian heartthrob, Roberto Carlos.

As the great day drew nearer, Marciano became a total outcast. His wife and her sisters had spread the word to everyone about the way he'd wasted their collective effort: months of painstaking handicraft. Not a dime was left to the household, the family hardly had a thing to eat, and although the machine made music, Marciano did not yet possess one religious record. He had not hired a band. His hearty animal soul must be wandering, sad and sick in the mountains somewhere, his wife concluded, for Marciano took on a ghastly green look every time he played his magic

—

machine. And yet he refused to see a curer, who might treat his animal soul and make Marciano well.

No one in the village could recall knowing a man who claimed he had to feel ill in order to discharge his sacred trust. How was it possible that such a fool could provide for the fiesta ? It was said that Marciano would not even allow his wife to purchase a religious record from the saleswoman who visited the village with so many wonderful items each Saturday.

"You'll wind up in jail for this," Marciano's wife advised him. They all faced ruin.

Messages went up the ladder of the village council, from mayor to alcalde, to the village elder. But as the tale rose through the ranks the officials were increasingly ashamed to pass it on in every detail. So, what the elder heard was, 'Marciano, who is entrusted with the duty of bringing us music for our next festival, has taken sick.'

The wise man paused after hearing this, indicating there might be some deeper significance in the inability of a trustee to perform his sacred mission. He ordered that Marciano immediately visit the curer, who could set his animal soul, and thereby his person, at liberty. When he appeared in the curer's hut, out of earshot of the magic machine with its four hit records, Marciano seemed instantly to be well. In the next days all eyes in the village turned thankfully to the curer.

During that time Marciano staunchly refused to accept any more help in providing music for the festive occasion. He allowed his wife and her sisters to decorate the small village square with bright hangings of crepe paper, to clean the ritual ceramics, to collect firewood and water. Tensely, the people of the village gathered on the great day, waiting in silence and in their appointed places beneath the colorful display. In the center of the village square a beautiful pavilion had been erected and the ground was covered with freshly cut pine needles. The structure seemed to tremble in anticipation, along with the Native Mexicans who surrounded it.

Finally, Marciano strode into the village square, moving toward the pavilion, his miraculous machine scratching a hymn to the Virgin of Guadalupe over the tight rubber grooves of the turntable. The villagers crowded around--tiny smiles you had to be a local to see curled the corners of the old women's lips, altering the weathered stone of their faces. Their tongues sounded musically with joyous, but gentle demonstrations. Yes, today there would be a fiesta, with much swaying and dancing, and flags waved by religious groups in honor of the saintly images they paraded.

Tomorrow, the people could face the endless labor of their looms, the immense piles of wood they'd carry for miles over the mountains, their tiny, stone-hard garden plots, with serenity. Why, it would even be remembered that the miraculous machine reproduced the exact sound of exploding fire-rockets !

The village jail cell would stay empty. Marciano had fulfilled his obligation. But the next day, while his wife fed him leftovers from the fiesta, as was the right of religious functionaries, Marciano told her, "I can only wish someone would bring us some fresh meat to show their appreciation. Good provisions are the best gift a man can receive."

Several months later, Marciano, a respected man in the community, still addressed by the honorary title of the office he'd fulfilled for the fiesta, but with more debts than money, set off, trotting down the jagged path back into the

—

city of San Cristobal de las Casas with the record player and four hits in his burlap sack. Though his wife had opposed the move, the period of his religious obligation was over. Marciano had argued--casting an eye over their parched, eroded land--there were mouths to feed.

It was easy for Marciano to find Juan Carlos, who sat like a conquering hero on one side of the central plaza, having his shoes shined. But when he spotted the Native and his misshapen burlap sack, the hero quickly got up and strode away. Running with short, rapid steps, Marciano caught up with Juan Carlos at the far corner of the square.

"I hope you're not going to try to sell that machine back to me after all this time," Juan Carlos said, nervously.

"Oh, no sir," answered Marciano. "I just wanted to thank you for a wonderful bargain. As you said--it was like a miracle!"

"You're saying that it worked ?"

"Oh, yes; it beautifully played a hymn to the Virgin of Guadalupe for our entire village and even made the noise of exploding rockets..."

"You don't say," replied Juan Carlos.

"Can I offer you a drink, sir, to celebrate the good fortune of my village ?"

"Why not friend? A drink! Vamos a copas," Juan Carlos responded. "I know a small bar right over there."

"But I couldn't allow that, sir," said Marciano, pulling full liter of aguardiente--firewater--from his sack.

About an hour and a liter later Juan Carlos said, "So you mean the machine actually made the noise of rockets, cannons, whistles, bugles--and tr-tr-trumpets too "

Marciano nodded his head. "Right your honor," he said. "We didn't even require a band."

After a hard bargaining session Juan Carlos managed to buy the magical record-player back from Marciano for the cash value of six embroidered Indian shirts, all the money he had left.

Marciano went back to his village that afternoon quite happily, with a brand-new machete and several other farm implements the family could use. Beginning with the next festival in his village a band always started the proceedings with Incense and Peppermint, playing on guitars, harps, carved flutes and gourd rattles. The music became so popular that townspeople came from miles away to attend fiestas in Marciano's village. They wondered who the poor villager was spending the day down by the little stream, looking as if he were about to be sick.

And Marciano would not have felt better had he known that, back in his little beige stucco house at the edge of San Cristobal de las Casas, Juan Carlos was never able to eke magic from the record player he had re-purchased, for he never tired of Petulia Clark's brash and brassy urgings to go Downtown.

—

Morning Coffee with a Political Junkie

Out in Carteret County, the suburbs were just beginning to drum up against the Allegheny Range. But talk was nothing new.

Longhaired Wes Dickens kicked off every morning at 7:30 with a cup of coffee and a look at the *Washington Post.* He had to drive up the narrow dirt lane from the house to the RFD box on the hardtop to get the newspaper, then quickly nose his little Toyota pickup back, and settle down in the kitchen. The local *Carteret Reporter*, for which Wes weekly wrote, was pushed to one side on the dining room table. *Post* things first.

It was September, and the time hadn't come yet for feeding split logs into one of the two state-of-the-art wood stoves that heated Wes and Mary's big old place. They had come to Carteret County from the city three years before. Mary was a top-notch nurse. She worked at the clinic every day.

Wes read the paper, did odd jobs, skillfully renovated their house while listening to talk radio or 24-hour non-stop news broadcasts, wrote his column and talked politics. From nine to five, about half of every hour was spent on political talk. Once dinner began, politics shot up to 100 per cent.

The phone rang. It was Sue Mullin, from over in Keeley.

"They're gonna do it, Wes..."

"Hey, Sue," Wes tossed the paper down. "What?"

"Looks like they're gonna build I-53 after all."

"Where'd you hear that?"

"Bill Morgan said it was tucked into that humongous transportation bill. Fuckers!"

"Porkers, straight from the barrel! Is he sure? It's a done deal?"

"He said it was buried somewhere on page 23."

"I'm not past the headlines. Shit! Now what do we do?"

"Watch the crowds arrive, I guess."

Sue Mullin had spent most of her free time during the last four years heading up a coalition to *Stop I-Five-Three*. Wes heard the air go out of her.

"I'll call Bill," he said. "Do you have time to talk to anyone?"

"Kids just left on the big yellow bus....I'll talk to whoever I can reach..."

"I'll call you back later," Wes said. "And take it easy. This ain't over yet."

I-53 wasn't the only fight on Wes' card. There also were: the industrial park--build it, but build it right, and the 3 out of 4 corrupt Carteret County commissioners--time to end their Good Ole Boy reign.

That was aside from the Everlasting National Scene and International Affairs, not to mention the Millennium: World That Just Might End. Wes Dickens' portfolio was always stuffed bursting full. Today, for example: greenhouse gases were up, the market was holding steady, and the President evidently hadn't had a hard-on for a little over a week.

Wes continued to page through the *Post* while the radio topically nattered away. Thought Wes: That god-damned highway! Who needs it? Who besides those two smarmy contractors who were Jessups and their three idiotic Finch nephews---the chainsaw happy roadbed clearing crew. OK, sure--good-paying work was a total necessity, but building interstates where a two-lane hardtop would do? There had to be a better way.

I'm lucky, is all, Wes reflected. Mary's good work at the clinic means I don't have to go at it full-time. Lucky me, lucky guy.

Wes threw down the *Post* and left a message on a machine for Bill Hearst, then talked to Frank Weems. They discussed the things that might be left for anyone to do about stopping I-53. A few details could be checked: sometimes the impact studies were stoppers: a done deal might not be a done deal, for all that. Then, getting Sally Porter's machine, he left the following message: "If all else fails, Sally, we can always chain ourselves to the rocks and trees in the blast zone." It wasn't necessarily a gag: Wes would have done it, thought he might do it, if need be.

Nevertheless, although he didn't want to admit it yet, on I-53, Wes felt they were beat. Whenever federal money trickled down in the form of construction gigs, you couldn't hardly argue against the people's sense that they were just getting their stolen tax dollars back. That was pretty near right! It was just another head-scratcher.

Now, there was that bookcase to install in Mary's study. Wes had prepared a nice space for it, about 6 feet wide. He had the shelves and supports cut; the pile of lumber was neatly laid out on Mary's floor. After everything else was done, the existing oak floorboards would be sanded and finished. Then the room, with its two new Thermopane windows showing off Sparrow Mountain to the east, and its bookcase nestled alongside Mary's antique roll-top desk, would really shine. Wes' work always looked great.

He picked up one of the unpainted vertical supports. The phone rang. Sue Mullin again. She's crying.

"I'm so damn mad!" she screams into the phone. "The road is going to come about 30 yards from us."

The Mullins lived what was still as yet pretty far back: four miles of dirt off old hardtop 53. They had nearly two hundred acres, a farm site and woods taking up an entire valley that seemed to exist outside of time. Ranging widely, about 30 head of lean, healthy cattle grazed at leisure. An ancient, nearly useless sawmill rusted under a tin-roofed shed; although Tom Mullin, working with Wes, did manage to get out some good-looking pine floorboard, some 14 months before--one hell of a task. Way back here, you still had room. Lord Fairfax himself would have admired Mullins' acreage.

"You'll still be a little ways from the road, won't you ?" Wes consoled.

"Not far enough. You'll always hear noise."

"I'm not saying it'll be better--"

"Fact is, it looks like the interstate will run just about right up the middle of us," Sue Mullin insisted.

"I guess—yeah, I remember the plans," Wes said. Not long before, he and Bill Hearst had been sent by the *Carteret Reporter* to Charleston, to see if they could bring any rough drafts of the road layout to light. Old Wales, the *Reporter's* publisher, felt educated opinion was suggesting a contract for a close survey had already gone out.

After he got back in the county with Bill Hearst, Wes had called Tom Mullin right about first thing.

"Shit," Tom said. "Horse manure."

At the moment, Wes was beginning to run out of things to say to Sue Mullin: he knew they were beat, that a big road was going to run right through the middle of her beautiful farmland, that it was as certain as the meat and potatoes it was going to put on a Jessup or a mindless Finch's table. Unless you were born a King, or the son of a mercantile Prince, you had to work to eat. Most of the local nobles worked even though they were loaded; so what could a commoner do?

"Shit," Wes now said to Sue. "We're gonna have to live with this sum-a-gun."

"Yeah, but not everyone will have it as bad as us..."

Wes was feeling frustrated. "Sue, I've been fighting right alongside you ever since I got here. What else can we do? I'm so sorry," he said. Sue was distressed, distressed for good reason.

"Wes," she began to cry.

"Holy crap, Sue," Wes cut in, "You don't suppose they drew it through your place just because you've been fighting, do you?"

"Everyone knows everyone else here," Sue answered.

"I'm afraid we're beat, Sue," Wes lamented. "We lost. Sum-a-gun."

"All those great columns you wrote against it..."

"Looks like they didn't make any difference. But I sure pissed some people off!"

"No kidding," Sue laughed.

"Look," said Wes, "We shouldn't give up altogether. But the handwriting on the wall is plain. Better get used to it."

"You're right. OK, Wes, then, I'll try to straighten up."

"Please take it easy."

Shit, it was close to eleven already. As for Mary's bookcase, Wes hadn't done a stitch.

He climbed back upstairs, and contemplated the stack of supplies on his wife's study-room floor. He picked up one unpainted vertical and nailed it carefully into a back corner of the bookcase space, then nailed up the other back corner support, checking meticulously to keep everything plumb. Next, he nailed up the left front piece.

Wes stopped for a moment when C-SPAN radio's non-stop coverage of the House judiciary committee caught

—

his ear. Impeachment hearings seemed inevitable by now: those smarmy Republicans wouldn't let up on Monicagate until they had eked the last dollop of advantage from it. Why hadn't that horny Clinton been capable of keeping his pants on!

Again, the phone rang. Running down the steps, Wes cursed himself for not letting the machine answer this one. He wasn't making much headway in Mary's study, and she'd be Queen Victoria royally pissed.

It was Bill Hearst, from the *Reporter*, wanting to tell Wes what he was hearing about Wes's "Our Last Shot to Kill I-53" column, which had run the week before. For months, while the highway debate raged, Carl Jessup had been known to be complaining loudly, every chance he got: at the Riley firehouse, at the counter in the Becker hardware store, over his beers at Dolly's. Of course, Wes knew that Jessup's wife was Old Wales, their publishers' niece. From time to time Wales would be making a call to Jessup, or somebody like him, to say how it made no difference, what Wes Dickens wrote, it was good for all of them to support free speech and laughing his "them dumb city fellers" laugh.

"Does make a difference to me," growls Jessup, who at six-five looks alarmingly like Paul Bunyan. "Makes me a tougher day."

"You can handle it, Carl Jessup," Wales tells him. "You're not so weak."

"....Longhair pains my ass."

"He's got a right to his two cents," opines Old Wales. "It's the American Way."

"Shove it," says Jessup. "I clear the way for roads. That's how I feed my folks."

"There will always be roads, Carl. Calm down..."

"Asshole longhair..."

Now Bill Hearst tallied it up for Wes: "Bet they're all down Dolly's gloating right now, those chainsaw hugging, dynamite toting, backhoe riding assholes. They got what they wanted again.. What else can you expect?" Bill was Carteret County born and bred.

"I expect that at some point they'll realize that they're fouling their own nests, Bill."

Hearst said, "In a little town, once upon a time …"

"Ya looked so fine, threw the bums a dime."

"Whut--what the hell are you talking about now?" Bill asked.

"You started in on a song..."

"OK, sure," said Bill. "But what now ?"

"Damned if I know," said Wes Dickens. "On that road, looks like we're beat."

"Sum a gun," said Bill.

Wes Dickens recollected when he had been arrested outside the U.S. Capitol, along with four Catholic nuns and sixteen other citizens, for peacefully demonstrating against the continued testing of nuclear weapons. When they laid down on the steps, police carted them off. Booked and released. They had won that one, you might say. If it came

—

to that, Wes would chain himself to a tree or a rock. Quickly and politely, he said goodbye to Bill Hearst.

Without a moment's rest, the phone rang again, a sound like the wake-up call of a malevolent genie. This time, Mary was calling from the clinic, and how pissed was she!

"You won't believe this," she says. "I'm fired. Sacked. The buggers. Looks like you're gonna have to go out and get some paying work for a while, Wes."

"Shit--what do you mean, you're fired?"

"The buggers say they're losing money..."

"And?"

"Just what I said: I'm fired. Any ideas?"

Wes thought of the interstate that would be impeding Mullins' cattle from migrating calmly, meditatively to their lower meadow. "I don't know what a good idea is today," he said to his wife.

"Anyway, for four more weeks I still work here," Mary alleged. "See you around 6:30."

"OK..."

"It was because you were always fighting them," Wes said to Mary, after she got back home and finished the story of how the company would shut the clinic. What could be done about that she asked rhetorically, checking some asparagus. Wes felt the sting of the words. These were the women in his life, he reflected. This was him.

"You can't fight all the time," he said.

"Shit, look who's talking about fighting," said Mary. She rarely cursed, and had to be in the nastiest mood.

"Get up, Wes," Mary was saying three months later. "It's 5:30, time to get going."

A mile from where Butch Finch and his crew were clearing for I-53, Wes was foreman on a three month contract to frame up a large structure that now sprawled like a dinosaur's skeleton alongside old S-53 hardtop, its raw ribs reflecting the sharp autumn afternoon sunlight. There the monster awaited resurrection on the land. It would be moved in sections, not far away, to a location where a curve of driveway could bring you in a minute or two from the coming interstate. Wes knew that what they were building constituted the frame of a motel and restaurant, and what would most likely become one or two shops.

For the moment, Sue Mullin was refusing to talk to Wes, although Tom understood: Mary would be out of work for a few months at least; their friends needed money to stay even, and that was that.

Drinking beer after work with a couple of buddies, Wes was several times heard to talk loudly about building the thing so it would fall down on top of some fool. But he didn't mean it, wouldn't have done it for reasons including the fact that, for all his rough edges, Wes Dickens was not capable of shoddy work.

"Sum a gun, somebody would likely get killed if the roof fell in!"

The chatter was the offspring of a few beers and the price of trying to keep the friendship of Sue Mullin and a few other folks.

—

"There's a feller does a lot of talkin'," somebody over at the pool table said.

"Writes that Commie opinion in the paper too."

"Not a boy from 'round home."

Meanwhile, behind the racket of their automatic hammers and Skill saws, Wes and his crew could hear the chainsaws and backhoes of the Finch boys a few hundred yards off. Driving in his truck with its outlandish, mud-encrusted tires, Carl Jessup passed their construction worksite several times daily.

He'd yell, "Sum a gun, you do good work, longhair!"

"Thanks a lot, Jessup!"

Mainly Wes kept his mouth shut, stuck with the job. It got on his nerves to have to work so nearby the Finch and Jessup crew, but really, what was the difference between them? Just a bunch of working stiffs...

"Fucking Finches," Wes was finishing the portrait of the workday for Mary over dinner. "How goes the deal for the new clinic ?"

Even before they closed the doors, Mary had been working to get backing for a new town healthcare site. Meanwhile, you had to travel about twenty-five mountain miles east or west, to Kinney or Richardson, to be seen in a hospital emergency room, as you had always had to before Mary came out to man the Carteret County Clinic three years earlier.

"Coming along OK," she said. "It looks like within six months we could be up and running again."

"That doctor--Peters--from Warrenville and his partners?"

"Looks that way."

"Meanwhile, I feel bad for your patients," said Wes.

"I have fifteen hundreds names in the files," Mary said. "Some of the elderly were really depending on not having to take that ride."

"Wish there was something more we could do..."

"Just don't catch anything I can't cure out of the upstairs medicine cabinet," Mary laughed. "But hey, not to worry. Peters and his group is just about signed up."

"Hurray for you, Mary, my wife," Wes said. "You're a local hero."

As the days wore on, Wes kept feeling that it was a royal pain in the ass to have to work so near the Finch-run roadway clearing operation. The sounds of chain sawing and dynamite blasts filled up any quiet moment Wes and his crew had. And then, from time to time, sounds of harsh cursing came from the excavation, under a mile away.

Somebody said, "Man---don't use it up all at once!"

Eventually Wes went to check what was going on.

Carl Jessup and Butch Finch were standing next to a newborn tree stump, looking over a chainsaw. Every couple of seconds, Butch Finch savagely kicked the machine.

"Longhair," Jessup said, "What the hay you doin' over here?"

—

"Just wanted to see what all the shouting was about," Wes explained.

"Botherin' you boys, are we?" asked Butch.

"No," said Wes, "Just curious about how that much noise is made."

Butch Finch gave his grounded chainsaw another swift kick. "Right now this here piece a crap don't want to work," he said. "Think I'll just bust the mother up..." He kicked the saw again, so that the blade spun.

"Come on, Butch," said Wes Dickens, bending over the saw. "That's no way to treat anything..."

"Don't you say!"

Wes went down onto his knees in the dust, to begin fiddling with the machine.

"Didn't say we needed your help, longhair," said Carl Jessup. "Did we Butch?"

After watching Wes work for a Carteret County minute, Finch elbowed him aside and grabbed up the saw.

"Just test it out now..." Wes said, steadying himself with an arm over the freshly manicured tree stump.

In Butch Finch's hands the chainsaw suddenly coughed and bawled, springing to life. He brought the blade down to cut directly thru Wes Dickens' wrist, leaving Wes's right hand sitting on the stump.

"Sum a gun, Butch," said Carl Jessup to his nephew. "Look what you done to the poor fool."

Wes got up, looked from Butch to Carl questioningly, opened his mouth and passed out against a pile of stones. Soon he was laid out in the bed of Jessup's pickup, his wrist wrapped tightly in a bloody blanket.

"You'll have to ride all the way to Kinney, ya know, Carl," said Butch Finch. "That there near-by clinic is close down."

"I know, Butch--I know. You make sure his hand is wrapped up good."

"Course I will."

Carl Jessup climbed into his monster truck. Then he was threading and bumping his way through the boulder-strewn roadbed, and climbing on up to old hardtop 53. It would take about 45 minutes to reach Kinney Hospital, and Jessup knew that Wes Dickens was bleeding bad.

The big-wheeled pickup nosed up the embarkment and shot off down the pavement, sprinkling gravel. After a lull moment, Mullins' herd of cattle began to amble down, heading for their beloved lower meadow, hesitating along the roadbed excavation line. A couple of the Finch boys whistled and hollered; their dogs barked. The cattle, as if exchanging thoughts above the noise of the coming interstate, milled and talked and attempted a decision, and stood still and went nowhere and still talked.

Miss Hap Goes to Paris

When I first heard them call my name on the radio I couldn't believe it, but there it was, large as life: Johnny Jones. They were saying my name after, "And the winner of the WTOP ten-day trip for two is..." That sound in my ears was like someone had chucked a big rock at my head, and I had to turn the radio off right away. But I turned it right on again to find out what they meant by the trip was for two.

"That's right, Johnny," said Mr. Bob Baker at the station when I called the next day, "it's all expenses paid for ten days in Paris or Hawaii, the place of your choice, with the person of your choice," he chuckled, "a lovely lady, I presume..."

"Beggin' your pardon," I said to Mr. Bob Baker, "but I think I'll have to go to Hawaii. I can't talk any French."

Somebody was laughing at the other end of the line, but I was sure it wasn't Mr. Bob Baker acting that way in a place like a radio station.

"That's fine, Johnny. Now, can you give me the name of your companion and the day you want to leave?"

"My what?"

"The person you want to share the trip with, you..."

I guess Mr. Baker wanted to call me a fool, but really I am not that bad although I was held back three times in the seventh grade, once in the eighth and it looks like again this year in the ninth if I keep up the way I been. I am told I am not a good student, but what can I do about that anyway? I guess I was smart enough to win this trip, and anyways, they say you don't really learn anything useful these days until college.

"Johnny?" Mr. Bob Baker was asking, "Can you give us her name so we can announce it on the air? I hope it'll be a surprise, because then, you see, we can get the girl on the phone live right after we announce her name..."

I told Mr. Baker that I didn't know any girls too good. He said hold on a minute and then asked for my phone so he could call me back pretty soon. It was Mr. Bob Baker again when the phone rang in an hour. He asked me how I liked this idea--would I go to France if they could find a girl who spoke some French by holding another contest on the radio? And she would go too.

"That's an idea," I told Mr. Bob Baker. "France is not Hawaii but it is somewhere near Paris."

"Right, Johnny. Now if you start listening to your radio tomorrow you'll hear the contest announcement for your co-winner."

"I can't. Tomorrow I got school."

Some noises like laughter came out of the room where Mr. Bob Baker was again, or maybe that was just my radio. But he told me it was OK, they'd call me to come in and meet the girl who won the contest to see if we could get along.

I didn't set a chance to listen to the radio for a couple of days but sure enough if they didn't call me anyways, saying they wanted me to come in to the studio.

—

They were gonna introduce me to three girls named Jessica Laing, Judy Tearsmith and Veronica Hap.

When I got to the station I got surprised cause I had never seen where that place was 'tho everybody said there was a tall pole on top. It had a string of red lights going up so you could see it at night. But it's really a pretty small building and they took me straight down to the basement.

"Hee-r-e's J-o-h-n-n-y," said Mr. Bob Baker in a voice that sounded like somebody else's when I got down to this small bright-lit yellow room. On a radio they had sitting on a desk there was all this laughing. There was also three girls standing around, all of 'em older than me.

Mr. Bob Baker was talking into a mike, saying, "That's right, it's Johnny Jones, winner of the WTOP trip for two...Johnny's come in to our studio today to meet with three lovely ladies, one of whom will be spending ten days with him in Paris. Hi, Johnny..."

I wanted to go over and say hi to Mr. Bob Baker since I had never met such an important person, but 'tho I was sure he was talking to me he wasn't looking at me at all, but in the direction of one of these technical guys who loves to wear earmuffs even though it's almost spring vacation.

Then some-body was pushing on my back in the direction of Mr. Bob Baker. Mr. Baker started waving his hand at me and I knew I was finally gonna get a chance to talk him in person.

"Hi, Johnny," Mr. Bob Baker looked at me for a minute, and then it was like they chucked a big rock at my head again, or maybe splashed me in the face with some sulfur or acid cause my vision went all blurry. I said hi, but then Mr. Bob Baker started telling something to the guy with earmuffs.

After he was done telling that guy about the three lovely girls that could speak French and were lucky enough to get their names picked out of a revolving drum, and how in fifteen minutes he'd be able to find out which one would be Johnny Jones' co-winner (whatever that is) I heard a lot of noise that sounded like applauding. But there was no big crowd down in that room, just us and the three girls, so I figured it must be the radio on top of the table.

I guess I forgot to tell you that Mr. Bob Baker had told the names of the three girls and which was which, but I really couldn't see any difference. Someone once said all girls are basically the same and if these three was any example I think the idea's accurate.

Now Mr. Bob Baker had put down his microphone and was talking to me, pushing me over to the girls and wanting me to meet them better. Every so often, 'tho I liked Mr. Bob Baker and was real glad to meet him, he would stop talking me and look over at the technical technician. This didn't make me feel too welcome, but after all, I thought, a radio station is not Hawaii or Paris.

Talking of Paris, it was funny, 'cause every other thing these three girls said was in French, I guess. I asked Mr. Bob Baker if he could speak it but he said not really and looked over again at Mr. dressed-for-winter. So I tried talking to the girls which was all acting friendly gathered close around me, putting their warm hands on my arm in that little room. But you don't learn enough subjects for conversation until the second half of the ninth grade or maybe the tenth I hear, and everything I said these girls would smile and answer French and then giggle just like Mr. Bob Baker's radio on the table.

—

"He don't have on his gloves," I said Mr. Bob Baker as a sort of joke, cause Mr. earmuffs the technician was holding up a hand with two fingers.

"Right," said Mr. Bob Baker. He reached over to the desk to pick up his mike again and whispered to me, "Now which one do you like, Johnny?"

I said I didn't know as long as they kept talking French couldn't tell nothing.

"Well, you know..." said Mr. Bob Baker I guess to me but he was looking at the technical technician hold up one finger.

"Which one looks good to you?"

"Looks good for what?" I asked Mr. Bob Baker. "They all got nice warm fingers."

"Oh, you know, don't you, you..." There I got the idea that Mr. Bob Baker wanted to call me a fool again but he wasn't even looking at me and was awful nervous.

"Sure I know," I told Mr. Baker. "But I forgot their names."

By the time Mr. Bob Baker had told the names of Jessica Laing, Judy Tearsmith and Veronica Hap again and which was which, the technician's face and got so red he had to take off his ear muffs.

He said just one thing, "Hurry."

Mr. Bob Baker talked into his microphone, "And now, Johnny Jones, who'll be the luckiest of these three?

Who'll be the girl spending ten thrilling days in Paris with Johnny Jones, all expenses paid by radio WTOP?"

There was a noise like a police siren all around me, coming from everywhere, so that it was worse than getting hit in the head with a rock or splashed in the face with acid, no matter what that dope Billy says about the worst way to get killed.

And then Mr. Bob Baker was saying, "Will it be Miss Jessica Laing, Judy Tearsmith or Veronica Hap?"

As long as that police siren kept going I couldn't remember a thing. I forgot those girls' names just as soon as Mr. Bob Baker told them. I looked confused at him but he stepped from girl to girl and said, "Will it be Miss Laing, Miss Tearsmith, or Miss Hap?"

Each one would smile at me lovely.

"Miss Hap," I said, cause it was the only one I could remember. After that I must have fainted or something cause all I can say is Mr. Bob Baker was shouting "Miss Veronica Hap" and the loud wailing of the police siren was getting closer 'til it nearly shook the radio off the table.

Well, that ain't the end of my story or the worst part or the best either. Cause when we got on the plane and got to know each other I could see that Veronica Hap was a pretty nice girl, and I had a pleasant feeling. When she didn't speak French Miss Hap kind of reminded me of one of my teachers in school, 'tho since she was twenty-four goin' on twenty-five I guess she was a little bit younger. But not too much older than me who am almost nineteen and besides she had what I heard called a nice figure.

—

"With all the French you know I bet we're gonna see a lot of Paris," I said to Miss Hap. We'd been flying in the plane already a couple of hours.

"I can't wait to get out of the hotel and onto the streets, Johnny," Miss Hap said. "It's such a beautiful city you will hardly believe it."

"You already been?"

"Oh yes Johnny, I lived there all last summer."

"And what kind of stuff do they have?"

Miss Hap smiled at me, "Do you like nice pastries?"

"Yeah." I didn't say for that we got all kinds of good stuff at home like Twinkies. Like I said, I'm not that bad. "What else do they got?"

"A really extensive metro system. You can go anywhere on it," said Miss Hap.

"Well, if it's extensive I ain't goin' near it," I told Miss Hap. She laughed.

"What's so funny?"

Miss Hap looked at me real close. "Oh nothing," she said. "It's just that they've given us quite enough money. We really don't have to worry one bit about how much we spend."

"That's good, and what else?"

"Plenty of museums," said Miss Hap, "surrounded by beautiful gardens. And all kinds of good food."

"I'm stayin' away from cemeteries, Miss Hap. But I sure am ready to eat. In fact I didn't have to wait for Paris or France or wherever it is to get a meal cause they were serving us all something on a little tray right there in the plane.

Meanwhile I said to Miss Hap, "One thing worries me 'tho, it's that record of activities they want us to keep for the radio station. I don't think I'm gonna remember all we done. If you'll excuse me for talking with my mouth full."

"Don't worry about it, Johnny," said Miss Hap. And that was all she said until the plane came into land.

We took a taxi to a sort of grey building with a green roof, which was where the driver went after Miss Hap told him the name of our hotel in French. It started to rain while we was in the cab and Miss Hap was bending over near my window like to touch the streaming crops.

I smelled like some flowers.

"Blah-blah-blah-blah," said the taxi driver.

"Blah," answered Miss Hap sitting up straight.

"What?"

"Oh..." said Miss Hap, "He just said, 'You speak good French! and I said, 'thank you'."

That was pretty good, if you ask me but not only this Miss Hap did but got us up to a beautiful room where there was two big beds and a real nice view with green rooftops. Then she said she wanted to go out.

"Boy," I couldn't wait to see the place. "I'll get ready with rubbers on in a minute."

—

Miss Hap said she wanted to go out for a walk by herself since it was already late on Sunday, and we'd start looking around the places that would be open Monday real early.

I felt like jokin' I didn't want to visit office buildings, but something was hurtin' so I carried my rubbers in the bathroom and called out, "I don't think you're gonna have too much fun walkin', Miss Hap, since it's still raining. Even 'tho it's Sunday there must be some place open."

Then my rubbers was on and I came out to see that Miss Hap was gone from the room. So I sat down there on my bed a minute feelin' funny and must've fell asleep cause the next thing was a real sunny light coming through the curtains and me still in clothes and my feet hangin' off the end of the bed still in rubbers.

And here's where comes the worst part of my story cause of the ten days trip I won Miss Hap was gone something like five. I never seen her or heard nuthin" from her in all that time. One lucky thing was each of us had got from the station their own stack of funny French bills.

So after a while the first day I took off my rubbers and went on the street. It was such a pretty place I figured I wouldn't been better off in Hawaii where at least I could have swimmed and talked and been said to, too. When the sun was shining like Miss Hap said Paris was full of all kinds of beautiful colored flowers and green trees. I even took a ride on this subway thing she mentioned and if I can figure right it wasn't all that extensive. But there was always people bumpin' into me and sometimes getting real mad like when I got ice cream spilled, so then I'd give some bills and make a signal like forget the change. In this way I met some nice folks but there was nothing I could tell or them say me. So nobody much long stuck around.

I wanted to walk a lot anyways and did but after a couple of nice days there was one where it rained pretty heavy. I got stuck in then and the next day when it rained again bad. That made me feel pretty lousy cause no one at all in the hotel would say me a thing and even when I offered them money to pay a meal or stuff they'd ask more and it seemed like rude.

I was wonderin' where Miss Hap went or if someone stole her suitcase or if she was killed and how I would get home then but funny cause she called that night.

"Johnny?"

"Is that you Miss Hap?"

I thought I could hear that she was crying, but maybe it was the rain outside.

"Johnny," she said, "Are you going to be in tonight?"

"Yeah. As long as this rain keeps I'm stuck up."

"Good. Then I'll come over and we'll talk, all right?"

"OK, but just don't try saying much French," I said, but I think before that Miss Hap hung up.

I was right to think her suitcase was stole or something cause she had it when she came in and if you looked close I think I was right her face had been cried. In fact she sat down on the foot of my bed and said me "Johnny" and then started to cry again.

"Whatsa matter, Miss Hap?" I asked.

—

"Oh, Johnny,"

She was crying so hard I went to shut the window cause I remembered the rain outside and the carpet could get wet.

"Miss Hap," I said, "I was worried about you some but I figured you must be havin' a wonderful time with everything so nice in Paris and the way you talk French."

But Miss Hap just cried and didn't say nothing.

So I asked again, "Whatsa matter?"

"He threw me out," Miss Hap said.

"Threw what?"

"Pierre," said Miss Hap. "He threw me out of his house. The lout."

I was trying to get the handle on this stuff I didn't too good understand when the phone rang. Miss Hap ran to pick it up and said, "Oh, Pierre" and then "blah-blah-blah" and was quiet.

Then she started to blah-blah again and after about fifteen minutes of this she started more to cry. I guess it was about half-an-hour of blah-blah-blah, crying and quiet before she put the phone down.

"That's it," Miss Hap said me. "It's all over with Pierre."

"Did they spill something on him?" I asked Miss Hap, but instead of talking she threw herself down on the bed near me and did not stop for one hour to cry.

About the same time the rain let up and I asked Miss Hap wouldn't she feel better if we went outside and she could cry there. She smiled and said:

"That's sweet Johnny, sure, let's take a walk."

We went out and all these big, beautiful blocks they call bulovas in Paris was gleamin' pretty with pavements slicked down and trees dripping rain. These outdoor places where people eat had all their chairs folded upside~down on top of the tables but we got to sit inside one. Miss Hap ordered us a fine meal.

And here the best part of my story starts to begin. I learned a lot then and the last couple of day with Miss Hap in Paris must've been like Mr. Bob Baker and the guys at the station thought they would been. It confused me at first 'tho, cause Miss Hap told me she'd be frank with me who everybody knows is Johnny.

"Ok, Johnny," she said. "No more jokes. I owe you an apology, and I'll start by telling you what happened with Pierre."

I didn't good understand any of this words, but I just answered, "Yeah."

"Pierre was my beau last summer when I was here," Miss Hap said. "And I hoped I'd win the contest so I could come see him again."

I looked confused cause I couldn't figure this stuff about a bow and how something got spilled all over with it and it was called Pierre. I guess I just sat there and opened my mouth a little like I sometimes do. But, like I said, I'm not that bad. I put a piece of food in real quick.

—

"Your bow?" I asked Miss Hap.

"Oh, dear..." said Miss Hap and explained me better all about Pierre and a few extra things.

We got along real good then 'tho there was only a couple of days left. Miss Hap showed me something I hadn't before done but she knew how to do it real good and I gotta say you it's pretty much fun. Then, before we waved goodbye at the airport, she said maybe I should get in touch and we could meet up and talk some French.

"Forget it," I said, so I was surprised a couple or so months later when Veronica (that's what she said to call her) phoned up me.

"How are you, Johnny?" she asked.

"OK, good...you?"

"Well...I wanted to know if you went in and talked to Mr. Baker at the radio station yet about our trip?"

I had forgot complete.

"That's fine," said Veronica. "Because I'm with child."

"I don't know him," I said. "Who's Child?"

"That's a good question," said Veronica and laughed, but I was used to not good understanding her words.

Then she said, "I've got an idea. I'm going to have a baby you see, Johnny. I want to have the baby and then put it up for adoption. But I thought we could offer the station a chance to put our baby up for a beautiful radio station baby adoption contest, and that way we'd make some money."

I said Veronica I didn't good understand none of this but anyways I didn't much trust the radio no longer. So she was quiet a minute and I thought sure she's gonna cry but then she said, Johnny, don't worry, and suggested something that's why I'm here talking to you movie guys.

Now I got one more thing to say that's I guess none of this would have happened if I went to Hawaii. And what Veronica said me to tell you too: that Johnny is not Pierre but she has seen worse.

—

SOCCER ZOMBIES COMING SOON

"Men from the city find that cutting firewood can be a very pleasurable activity…" Lei Lo Li

Margaret Stokes, formerly Margaret Miller, while pretending not to carefully follow the flow of her son Scott's soccer match, had her fingers crossed inside the right-hand pocket of her slacks. Boys in green and purple uniforms surged and clotted around the checkered ball. Wham: low to the ground, Scott whirled out of the pack, heading for the goal. Moving the ball from right to left, he beat one, then another, little defender. He had an instant to stop, to consider the goalie. Scottie read uncertainty and fear of parental disfavor in the keeper's eyes, which were adequate to tarnish the opponent's concentration. That was the signal for Scott to rocket the ball into the upper right-hand corner of the net. Goal!

In fact, nine-year-old Scott Miller was at home, in bed, two sleeping pills being more than enough to put his sixty pounds down. But the action on the field of play was not Scott's dream.

Beginning in the 1940's, Margaret's mother Kay Crosby, practically speaking the first woman bush pilot in Alaska, had effected 72 recorded rescue operations, responding to avalanches and swift weather changes. People in the territory said that, in fact, she must have been in on at least twice as many saves.

Kay would tell Margaret how she was actually the one who spotted a crippled fishing boat off Kodiak Island, and that she had flown circles, running low on fuel and without a working radio in dense weather, to guide a Coast

Guard cutter to the distress area. Kay married an intrepid Coast Guard officer, Ken Miller, who was decorated for his part in rescuing the boat's crew of eight half-frozen men. Captain Miller was transferred to a highly valued intelligence desk at Langley, and he carried Kay, sinewy and suntanned with her brown pageboy and burning black eyes, kicking and screaming across the threshold of their new home in McLean, Virginia. So it happens that, apart from the birth of the couple's daughter Margaret in 1951, we will never know all there is to know of Ken Miller's exploits.

We do know that a Romanian immigrant named Nestor Velo arrived in the United States sometime in the early 1980's. Sporting a paisley cravat, he set up shop as an art dealer in the vicinity of Dupont Circle. Velo appeared to prosper, marrying a Washingtonian, and later traveling frequently to Paris to tend a second gallery in the Rue de-, and to purchase newly liberated, but previously quite obscure, Eastern European artwork.

Before long Velo was being run by agent Ken Miller. The art world scuttlebutt that said Nestor Velo never paid his Eastern Europeans was a real screamer because there were no Eastern Europeans to pay; the CIA slipped Velo money to fund a few adept copyists in Transylvania who told each other tasteless jokes in their local idiom about 'blood money' and went back home to restore the castles they had bought at auction.

As a native Alaskan, Ken Miller knew about, and believed devoutly in, the edge. Hell, the edge was at the American core like the core of apples for apple pie, he figured in simile, although the edge was what so many liberal softies had forgotten. (Too many Mrs. Whoever's cakes out of a box for most of us, perhaps?) Nowadays, on the wrong side of the aisle, they preferred to act as if

—

nobody was better than anybody else, mused agent Miller, strapped in front of his scintillating bank of sixteen screens.

His ability to work with conviction was why Miller had substantial control over anywhere between 12 and 15 long-playing field assets like Nestor Velo at any given time, people fresh from the provinces and looking for a leg up. *Fresh Fields,* what an idea, Miller thought: America the Best.

Although he had been told to keep hands off Latin America, the ghoulish and debonair Velo was the first to bring up certain facts. Did Miller know there was a market for street kid 'cadavers,' in point-of-fact cryogenically preserved and lab-certified, after having been disposed of by flying death squads of off-duty Brazilian cops?

"I am aware of the fact that Rio and Sao Paolo police are liable to moonlight in marginal what you might call clean-up ops," Miller says.

"Where do you suppose the little ones go?"

"To the bottom of a canyon below a hillside favela or in some open lime pit, would be my assumption."

"Yes, and others have been captured alive or picked up--just recently killed and then subjected to procedures, that I have been told are---state-of-the-art," says Velo.

"Rumors, aren't they?" says Ken Miller, fighting the terrible thrill. What God-forsaken art are you talking about now, he thinks. "What's the use?" he asks.

"I can discover..."

Back in McLean, Scott Stokes and his mom Margaret are visiting Grandma and Grandpa. These days,

Kay Miller, still lean as a greyhound, cultivates roses in her greenhouse, tends her stamp and coin collections, and raises funds for Republican Senate candidates from the states of Virginia, North Carolina and Tennessee.

Everyone knows better than to talk shop with Ken. You talk about yourself and sometimes you get a nice surprise. For about fifteen minutes Margaret has done nothing but tell her folks about Scott's soccer team, which is 0 and 4. During the last couple of minutes, Scott has cried. House rules state: he can't get up and go away without being excused.

"Can that coach be an absolute idiot?" asks Kay, putting down a teacup.

"There's nothing we can do about *him*," Margaret says.

"Could it be that the other teams in Scott's league are more talented than they were last year?" Ken asks.

"Maybe—half of the boys seem to be from Cameroon or Mexico or someplace exotic," says Margaret.

Here Scott comes up for air. "They're too good," he says.

Kay insists that Scott quit crying immediately. She takes his hand in her hand.

To follow up on Nestor Velo's intelligence, Miller chooses Lucky Numbchux, a Cariblanasian from Colombia who contains more races than Tiger Woods. Numbchux can operate seamlessly in his home country, in Peru, Ecuador and Brazil.

—

Lucky picks up the scent of a renegade lab forty miles up the Rio Negro from Manaus. The place is only accessible by boat.

"All is goo," he informs Ken Miller, since the d key on his mini-laptop sticks.

Employing tried and tested James Bond tactics we have not been treated to in movie theaters, Numbchux penetrates the hidden lab complex. Built on pylons, hive-like platforms extend over acres of floodwater, just 50 yards from the majestic Rio Negro. Vines and lianas hang in profusion from elegant trees, and lily pads float everywhere in this lovely sanctuary, originally constructed as the *Amazonian Lotus Retreat.* However, a malaria outbreak soured prospects for eco-tourism at this spot.

It appears to Numbchux that the new owners are most likely offspring of Dr. Josef Mengele who have evaded Interpol detection, and they sure as shootin' aren't running any jungle paradise hotel.

Lucky does his best to maintain a low profile.

Margaret calls her Dad. She sounds upset.

"Bill will be coming home," she says. "What's he going to think?"

"Margaret---about what?"

"Scottie stinks !"

"Can it be that important?"

"To his Dad? It sure as heck is."

Recalling Martin Sheen aiming to kill Col. Kurtz and painted like a local native with the phosphorescent coloring of an unknown bird, Lucky Numbchux now surfaces slowly from the murky backwaters of the Amazon, The boss would be happy with him; he is at the edge. He makes his way to an outlying unit. Formerly designated the Pantera Onça Suite, one of twelve of the inn's unparalleled Amazonian Denizen Luxury Class, the building is now known as Site Three Z.

Lucky peers with his special field optics through the smoked glass. The Colombian, who, previously outfitted with a racing motorcycle, has thrown bombs into the cars of honest judges and terrified journalists in Bogotá and Medellin, creating bloody messes on behalf of Pablo Escobar, is inured to the ghastliest sights. Nevertheless, tonight Lucky senses that he is witnessing the unmentionable. He wonders how Langley will view his 6 a.m. update.

Shortly after strapping himself into position in the morning, Ken Miller is a little disgusted when he takes in the details. But he is never at a loss for an idea.

"Find out how they can be revived," he messages Lucky Numbchux, who for the moment, has retreated to the safety of Manaus. "And see if you can get one out for us."

"All of this may take various days…"

"You have a green light and the usual per diem plus extras, Lucky."

"We are goo," Lucky sends back, vowing to get his laptop fixed ASAP.

—

A week later the package arrives at Langley. It is placed in storage while Ken Miller reads the rudimentary manual, which Lucky composed after extracting several drops of honey from his keyboard.

The little man finds a home in Ken's garage, where a process dedicated to turning him into a replica of Scott with King Hell soccer talent will take place. This will be time-consuming, because, among other things, the zombie Brazilian street urchin is twenty-past-midnight black. He needs to be programmed to speak English, and to live for nothing but Sponge Bob Squarepants and the trinkets you get from McDonald's, in addition to his inherent one or two goals per game. He has to forget about begging directly and learn to favor emotional blackmail. He must cease to try to go places on his own, and learn to ask Grandpops for a ride. This happens in due time since Ken Miller is a masterful trainer, and has, for the skin-color challenge, access to some not yet ready for the supermarket varieties of bleach and dye.

Late on a subsequent Saturday morning, Margaret is dragging little Scotty along.

"You let that kid go right around you," she says.

"Mom, we just stink."

"I'll say. You sure do…"

Scottie doesn't know what to say. But he holds his tears back.

Margaret talks to Kay that night. "Mother, I don't know what to do. They're 2-6 now. When Bill gets back from Russia, he'll flip."

"Margaret, have you ever known Bill Stokes to roll over and play dead?"

"Actually, I'm beginning to forget what he looks like."

"It's the life we've chosen, daughter. But you don't want to be too hard on Scott."

Ken Miller keeps very few family secrets from Kay. He chooses this time to show her what he has in the garage. By now Zombie Scott looks more than somewhat like their grandson. He can be awakened easily on command. Thanks to Ken Miller's talents as a trainer, the zombie's language skills are coming along. Soon, he will be able to fit right in.

When they come through the garage door the zombie is indulging in a ritual he has brought with him from Brazil. Authentic materials not being readily at hand, he has made various adaptations. Instead of a plaster Saint George, a plastic Lion King is at the center of his altar. He couldn't find chalk, so with magic marker, he drew circles on the spot where Ken's Mercedes is normally parked. He has five candles placed within the circles, all at strategic positions. Where popcorn is strewn about macumba circles in Brazil, Zombie Scott has likewise scattered popcorn.

"Fascinating," says Kay. "What do you suppose it means?"

"Why not ask him?"

"What's the meaning of this, young man?"

"I score more goals."

"He's precious, Kenneth."

—

Ken still has some tough ones to figure. If he tells Margaret, she'll know it's not her son that did it. If they tell Scotty, he'll…if they don't tell him, well, go figure.

But Margaret agrees to be all go for the glory. The zombie is a willing minion. That leaves Scotty. Putting him to sleep during the games seems to be the ticket. He'll wake up and they'll say he was awesome, as good as Pele, Cruyf, Maradona or Messi; it must be that he goes into a Zone, and doesn't remember all the quality stuff he does.

With the season half over, Scott is told he now must have a nap before every game. He wakes up later. He is told how great he was. The team draws even: 6-6. The zombie is the best nine-year-old player anyone has ever seen. Scottie learns to bask in glory, claiming he remembers nothing. It's working.

Only, one time Scotty didn't fall asleep right away. He got out of bed and went to the window. He saw Grandpops remove this Scott doll from the trunk of Mom's Wrangler. It actually walked, got into the passenger seat, and fastened its safety belt. Scott saw them drive off, toward the field. Then he blacked out.

When Scott woke up, he remembered these things. His plan was to pocket the sleeping pill on the coming game days. He wondered what they were doing with that model of himself.

The next Wednesday night, they were visiting Grandma and Grandpop's. The grownups were talking.

Mom said, "Bill will be back in three weeks…"

"That's great—he'll be here for the finals."

"Among other things," said Margaret Stokes.

Scotty drifted to the garage. He went in and awakened the zombie.

"Glad to meet you," said the Brazilian.

"I hear you're an awesome soccer star," Scotty told him.

"Well, yes, you know that I'm Brazilian."

"I wish I could play like that."

"I could try show you."

"But aren't you like—dead?"

"I don't think so. I just have to sleep a lot."

"That's the same thing they say to me!"

A clandestine practice session was held on the spot. Scotty could improve, but how much? Meanwhile, they talked.

"Your life sounds terrible," Scottie told the zombie. "And you're sure you aren't dead?"

"I don't feel so."

"I feel so, sometimes," Scottie said. "You keep on playing on Saturdays," he told the zombie. "They won't realize I know about it, and I doubt if they would care."

The zombie considered Scotty's expression. "You don't feel very well over this?"

"Sure—not really."

—

"I am sorry, Scottie. Oh, one more another thing: Did you know how I have come here to this place?"

"Not really," said Scottie.

"I have been trying to find it out, but…"

"Tell me what you do know," Scottie said.

"And that's it, Grandma," Scottie says to Kay Miller on another afternoon.

"Trying to make your Mom happy, is all," she says. "Sometimes compassion can skip a generation too."

"What, Grandma?"

"Sorry, Scott, I'm thinking aloud."

The day after arriving home following two months' assignment in Moscow and spending the requisite time with his wife in the sack, Colonel Bill Stokes stands on the sideline of the soccer field, in uniform alongside his wife Margaret and the other excited parents. Scotty's squad has beaten teams with better regular season records, and advanced to the final match. Now they face Purple Haze, the favorite. Scotty has played like mad, dashing all over the field, controlling the ball, making perfect crosses, dribbling with panache, attacking the goal again and again. But purple's defense is packed in tight, and they lead 1-0, with two minutes left.

"Come on Scotty, come on," yells Margaret Stokes. She has no doubt that the zombie will come through.

Back in the Ken Millers' garage, the Lion King is at the center of the macumba circle, waiting patiently. Five big candles glow. Popcorn is showered over the dusty floor.

Kay Miller--home that morning with, "I'm sorry dear, just a terrible migraine"--sits cross-legged, whispering something like a prayer. The zombie sleeps.

"I've got your plane ticket right here," Kay whispers to him. She thinks of that day in the 1940's off Kodiak Island, of the five shivering men standing in the glacial rain on the deck of Ken Miller's cruiser, thanking him for saving their lives. How that handsome Coast Guardsman took all the credit for the rescue, stealing her glory scene.

"It won't happen to you, I promise," Kay reassures the zombie. "I'm sending you home where you can once again be a nameless orphan and run free, one step ahead of the police."

Zombie Scott's head nestles in her lap; Kay strokes his temples while he sleeps his fathomless sleep. She has come to love him as her own.

—

Frankenstein Meets The Behemoth, or A Likely Story

"Well?"

"I don't know," said Murray, "How about a drink then?"

"Sure," I said, grabbing for my pea coat, "Let's go."

We went down the stairs and out onto W. 12th. The night air held that dreadful Winter chill, but it didn't really matter. We were on our way to the bar, and the Bistro was just around the corner.

On W. 4th I said the same thing I always said or thought, after rounding the corner, "That's where Jana lives," I said, "You know, she Timmy's girlfriend. You remember, we met Tim on the street here, just the other evening."

"He seemed like a nice fellow, that Tim," Murray began, but by that time we had reached the Bistro. We went through the double doors into a measure of human warmth. Faces of the regulars lined the tables near the window, familiar faces at the bar. I looked around.

"A brandy," Murray went directly to the bar. He turned around to ask me.

"And...what will you have?"

"The usual."

"A brandy and a beer then." Murray took his drink from the bar, examining it, smiling. "Cheers," he said, tipping his head, with the blonde Viking locks back.

"Cheers." Right away I felt a little more solid. Knocking back a few with Murray was so natural.

I said, "I wish I could be happier here in New York when I'm not working."

Murray said nothing. He sipped his brandy. Then with a look of reproof, he said, "Well, you'll be off pretty soon, won't you then?"

"That's right," I brightened.

"You'll be back in sunny Rio with all those lovely women..." Murray smiled wickedly over the top of his half glass of brandy. "Things can't be all that bad."

"That's right, mate."

We both turned in our seats as the door opened. It was the habit of the place that everyone looked up when the doors opened, hoping to see something new and special. This time the doors opened and a couple walked in, followed by a draft of cold air.

He was short and had curly hair; she was a chunky, obviously bleached blonde wearing a black leather jacket.

They pulled up to the bar on our right.

"Well, well." I nodded at them, looking past Murray.

—

"What's the matter with you, mate?"

"Nothing; she looks better than I thought. Ya know." The woman exuded a rough appeal, diverting me.

"You're just another wolf brains," Murray said.

"I guess. Then, how's Peter?"

"Fine," said Murray. "Home in New Zealand."

Behind my back a small knot of people was gathering, edging toward the bar in the orbit of the blonde. Somebody brushed past my shoulder and called the bartender for a drink. I turned around a saw a fellow in a green sweater with a drink in his hand, near the door. A buddy of his started talking with the blonde's partner.

I asked, "So you think you'll be around New York for another two months?"

"Probably...then, I'm not sure just what I'll do. Want to stay away from Sydney." He gazed off.

"Well, look at Frankenstein," said the blonde woman behind me. She sounded drunk. There was a trace of interest in Murray's eyes, and the start of a motion to get up off his stool. With that, someone bumped my back, jolting me slightly forward, towards the bar. I moved to turn around.

"Finish your drink." Murray was facing the bar. "It's just that loopy woman."

Behind us, in the center of the barroom floor, a scuffle was developing. I turned around to watch it. The blonde's man was shoving against the fellow in the green sweater, who looked like a German, strong and stocky. Green Sweater was being held back by his friend, who wore a raincoat and in fact, looked like Frankenstein.

"Now she's done it." I turned to Murray, "She really ought to know better than to call a guy who looks like Frankenstein, Frankenstein."

Murray couldn't help but laugh, so I went on.

"She doesn't seem to have learned the basic lesson of life," I guffawed, watching the tussle. "The secret is always to dissemble, never to tell the truth..."

"Turn around and finish your drink, mate." Murray said. He couldn't keep from chuckling. "You're enjoying it, aren't you? You wanker."

By this time the tussle had reached quite some proportions behind us, what with the stocky German trying to kill the blonde's man and Frankenstein holding him back. The bartenders sprang into action as bouncers along with the regulars, defending their territory. A shoving match, developed, spinning around the amber barroom. By the door, bouncers and a couple of regulars were waiting.

"Get out."

"And stay out, you guys, if you don't want any more trouble."

—

The regulars straightened their hair, pulled up their pants, and wiped their hands clean, re-entering the Bistro.

"Can't believe it," said one, shaking his head.

Murray confided to the black cook, "Look, if you don't want any more trouble, you'd better throw that blonde out. She's the cause of it."

"You're right," said the cook. "She's bad, all right."

The woman was dusting off her boyfriend's leather jacket. She was explaining herself in a whisper.

"Throw 'er out," Murray admonished the cook, then he turned to me.

"You see what I mean? About her, that blasted woman was the cause of it all. And you really enjoyed it, you did," said Murray.

"Listen, it was you getting involved. I didn't turn around to fight, just to keep from getting hit from behind. You jumped in, like all the rest."

"That bloody woman," said Murray.

I said, "Look maybe we'd better change the subject. Now that it's over."

Then the Bistro doors opened again. Green Sweater walked in, followed by Frankenstein, They walked to the center of the room.

Doug, one of the bartenders, immediately went to the end of the bar to phone the police. Meanwhile the other bartenders negotiated with Frankenstein and Green Sweater in the middle of the room. One held a thick club.

"They've come back," Murray gloated. "You can just hear what they're saying. Sickening, conciliatory things, you know. Bloody Hell, this makes me retch. They're pleading."

Frankenstein and friend stood in the center of the room, trying to make amends. But the bartenders wanted no more trouble. Over my shoulder the woman shouted insults.

"Shut 'er up...get 'er out," Murray pleaded.

"Poor guy," I said, "He's probably having to deal with the fact that he looks like Frankenstein every day. Imagine that. Really does look like Frankenstein."

"Shut it," said Murray.

A huge man in a blue coat and a blue knit cap came through the door and stood to one side of the bar, consulting with a few of the regulars.

"Look at this guy," I said.

"Yeah," Murray nodded, "He owns the place."

"Rough character—a regular Behemoth."

"Give a rest, will you?" Murray said.

—

The police arrived with negotiations still in progress. Frankenstein and Green Sweater fiercely defended their right to a drink. The regulars were telling their versions of the story. The blue Behemoth stood to one side, talking to a bartender, listening.

"This cannot be fair," said Green Sweater, sounding authentically German.

But it was no use. The police listened too, politely, not having much on their hands for the moment. Popular opinion was against Frankenstein, and eventually the police escorted the two out. There was a short conference in front of the bar, then Frankenstein and Green Sweater walked around the corner onto W. 4th, going towards 8th Avenue, making expansive gestures.

The police car remained, for a moment, on the corner of Jane Street.

"I imagine they told then," I turned to Murray, "not to show their faces here again tonight."

Murray nodded, "But it is really unfair, you know. I've got no sympathy for those two morons, coming back in here like that to whine. But they should throw these two out as well."

He motioned contemptuously over my shoulder. Behind me, the blonde was making time with another fellow, a tall, thin guy I hadn't seen before.

"See that?" cried Murray, "That witch."

"OK, look," I said. "Let's just get the hamburger for Mara and get out of here. I'm tired of this."

"There's an idea, mate. We'll get just one?"

"Right, she only wants one," I said.

"Spot on mate. One is enough," Murray motioned to the black cook.

"A burger to go," he said.

"You know what else ought a go." The cook frowned.

Murray lifted his brandy to toast that.

In the corner, the hulking Behemoth stood talking to Doug, who was nursing a cut on the heel of his hand.

"Go home if you need to," the Behemoth said.

"Thanks, boss, it's nothing," said Doug. "I'll get a band aid."

The regulars went on talking, gesticulating, and shaking their heads. Our hamburger arrived. Out we went, onto West Fourth.

It was cold out, really cold. I thought of Green Sweater and Frankenstein out walking in that frigid night. I looked up absentmindedly in the direction of Jana's apartment. I had never met Jana. It seemed there must be something to say, but the chill air displaced the scene in the

—

bar, leaving nothing. We went up the stairs, reaching the apartment in silence.

Mara had already gone to sleep, and she roused slowly, "What, only one hamburger?" she said.

"Well, you're half asleep anyway," I explained, trying to help. "And there was a fight in the bar. You see, Frankenstein and his German friend Green Sweater..."

"You guys forgot the ketchup," Mara whined sleepily, pulling the sheets back around her.

Murray took a bite from her hamburger.

"And you only brought one. I told you two because I know you'll want some of it," Mara rolled over onto her stomach.

"We'll go back out for the ketchup, OK?" Murray offered, putting the hamburger down on its plate next to the bed.

"All right." Mara was nearly asleep.

"Pretty stupid," said Murray when we came out onto the street again. "'Plenty of ketchup,' she said."

"OK, we'll be back there in a minute; it's right over here." Once again we walked in through the doors of the Bistro.

"Bloody Hell, what's this?" Murray held up his hands.

Half of the chairs and tables had been pushed over onto the barroom floor, or thrown against the bar. In one corner, the blonde was cowering in the arms of her new, slender lover. But the main event was on the floor.

"Maybe we'll have to forget about the ketchup," I said.

"Not a chance, mate. Come on," Murray stepped towards the bar.

Over in front of the bathroom floor, beneath a table, Frankenstein was out cold. A bartender and a regular had him pinned into a pool of urine, beer or blood (or all of the above) which spread out beneath him.

"He isn't moving," said Murray.

"Might be dead."

"Well," Murray exchanged a look with the black cook. "They shouldn't have come back."

Green Sweater, who hadn't been knocked unconscious, let out a terrible groan. In the corner, the blonde woman and her boyfriend spouted insults. Green Sweater kept groaning, periodically: horrible, agonized noises. Above him Behemoth towered mightily, frowning. Frankenstein's face was sweeping up the floorboards. His legs lay flat, and once or twice, he grunted. It sounded like the worst sore throat.

Each time he grunted a regular grabbed for his legs. Another gave him a belt on the back with the bar stick. This went on for couple of minutes until patrolmen walked in, two cars full, three troopers and a grumpy Captain.

Behemoth talked with him while the troopers flattened Green Sweater to the floor, handcuffing the poor fellow. Over in front of the bathroom Frankenstein lay dead to the world, bathing in fluids. A regular was seated on the floor at arm's length. Behemoth and the bartenders explained everything, though Behemoth had come in late, and didn't know the whole story.

"It's that bloody blonde they should take in," the cook confided to Murray.

"Didn't I tell you?" Murray turned to me.

I was watching Green Sweater, laid out in front of the doorway, flat on the floor, handcuffed and trying to turn his face upward to lobby the Captain. The police lifted Frankenstein up out of his puddle and trundled him towards the door, with the help of the Behemoth. They picked up Green Sweater, who suddenly began to shout and struggle.

"He won't give up," said Murray.

The police hustled Green Sweater out inside their little circle. Green Sweater bounced from one to another, groaning, then went limp into the arms of a patrolman.

"He really got it," I said.

"All right, everybody out," the police captain was saying.

"The Bistro is closing." The bartenders took it up, wiping the bar with their cloths, re-arranging the tables. Through the windows you could see the green and white patrol cars parked on the dim street, with the low brick buildings of the Village behind them. Frankenstein and Green Sweater were cloth dolls, draped over the trunk of one of the patrol vehicles, face down and handcuffed.

Murray turned to the bar, "On that hamburger...we forgot the ketchup."

The cook looked perturbed but handed over a half-empty bottle.

"Here, take it all," he said.

"Thanks," said Murray.

"Let's go, everybody out," the bartenders were saying. In the street the regulars talked in knots as we passed under Jana's window with the bottle of ketchup. With a sharp wind off the Hudson it was as chilly as a polar New Year's, and rounding the corner you missed the warmth of the Bistro.

—

Over Our Heads

"It's OK to be mixed up in stuff, Easy. You just gotta be sure you're mixed up to the top of it."

Tom Sizemore character, Devil in a Blue Dress

1.

The stately Georgian revival brick house on P St in Georgetown had a four-foot tall yellow and red metal abstract sculpture stationed out front. As it didn't quite go with the architecture, the metalwork made its point. See if I care, the piece proclaimed.

There at Peebles Fine Art, Elizabeth, a lithe blonde with a pageboy and oceans of calm prep school class, greeted you. Later such young ladies graduated to gallery operations under their own names. You could see that Elizabeth had what it took.

"Gail will be down in just a minute," said Elizabeth.

"Fine, I'll look at the show."

I walked around the big white room with the consummately polished oak floorboards. Each wall was hung with a panoramic photo of a Washington landmark, about ten feet wide by two feet high made with a camera that does a 360, capturing the surround and straightening it out. The Lincoln Memorial, the Key Bridge, the White

House and the Watergate: dizzying and spectacular takes on the familiar scene.

After ten minutes I offered to Elizabeth, "Strong!"

"Gail will be right down," Elizabeth said, nodding in agreement. "She's just finishing a call to the Mideast."

I always sport this look like I have a lot to learn. Sometimes I kid myself into thinking that's a handy disguise.

"Hello, Steven." From behind me, Gail Peebles' voice crackled like a prairie states station, full of static.

I'm Steven James, by the way. I wrote art criticism and worked as an independent curator with some success for over twenty years. Now I'm more into promotion. I was wondering now if doing a favor for Gail Peebles could make something momentous happen. There I was.

I knew Gail had been traveling to the Mideast quite frequently, doing things. She gave talks to junior Chamber of Commerce groups, fitted out new hotels in the Persian Gulf States with immense, colorful geometric-doodle paintings for their lobbies, and sold a pricey Old Master canvas now and then to a liberal sheik, who would show it to no one.

Gail was not uncomfortable with oil. Maybe that went for everyone from Texas, but Gail's money didn't come from oil wells, not her own. She excavated men. She

—

was a blonde dish prone to slit sheath dresses with stitched floral patterns, and she wore stiletto heels. The former Miss Dallas (late 70's) curves were beginning to buffer out, but Gail could still command the spotlight at 46. She was nuts, quite successfully so.

"How about these panoramic photos?"

"Nice show, Gail," I said. "Do you ever have one that's weak?"

She smiled primly and contentedly, and said with a baby doll voice, "Thank you, Steven."

We sat down at a round table near the front of the big room. Gallery fliers and invitation postcards were piled neatly there, next to the visitor sign-in album. This was the way dealers expanded their invaluable mailing lists.

"So—in your message you said you could use some help. Can't Elizabeth handle…?"

"No, I mean, yes—Steven! Liz doesn't have time for this! And I sure don't—running one way and another on this planet like I do. Thank God the boys are away at school. But I know you work fast, and you always seem to make time for important projects."

"What are we talking about?"

"You'd be taking on a contract with the U.S. Chamber of Commerce, helping us with some talks I will present…"

"One of those pro-biz trips?"

"Exactly, it's totally connected to that."

"Don't they have their own material for that kind of talk?"

"Yes, I mean--no. I have to adapt my talks to the arts. They don't handle those. It's more work than I can look at, and my next trip's coming up in ten days. Please, don't say no!"

"Sure Gail, show me some files."

Gail's cell phone rang. "I have to take this," she said. "But thanks a million. You're a sweetheart!"

She held out a white card from the Chamber of Commerce with contact info for Henry Constance, Cultural Liaison, lettered in red and blue.

"E-mail him right away," Gail said, pointer finger over her cell button. "Henry's a whiz; he handles every single thing." Her smile showed me the way out.

2.

The project was manna from heaven, considering the three thousand dollars that Henry Constance advanced. Boilerplate pro-business files from his office swiftly flew to my desktop, racing contributions from Elizabeth on Gail Peebles' exemplary life and work. I stitched these together into four separate 15-minute talks for Gail to deliver, adding material I could readily gather on the manifest importance of artistic endeavor. At the end of the process drafts would go back through Constance's office for revision, and head for the Emirates in Gail Peeble's laptop.

I was settling into my second morning's work on Gail's project when the telephone rang. It was Caspar Velo. Velo, a natty and courtly Romanian, had prospered dealing (post Berlin Wall) Russian and Eastern European artwork in all media, from portrait miniatures to monumental sculpture—wow! When some of his Glasnost era artwork looked so exciting, I'd curated a show for Velo and written a good deal of upbeat criticism. He made lots of money and gave many people gifts.

Then, trade scuttlebutt claiming that Velo never paid his Eastern Europeans artists started floating, and it was further said that there were no bonafide artists to pay. The big gag: the CIA was slipping money to a few adept copyists in Transylvania for propaganda—they wanted to be sure there would be fresh artwork coming out of the defunct Soviet Bloc that clearly didn't feature Lenin embracing some machine.

Washingtonian big fun of the Nineties you say, but meanwhile, Velo prospered. People bought what they liked, often after they had been told what they should like, and why. Breaking down the great mystery of images into serviceable words was where people like me figured. And yes, directly after the wall came down, the Eastern Europeans had a very fresh look and performed like great investments—but it *was true*--roughly half what was being touted as the work of "artists who gallantly survived under Communist oppression" *was* forged.

You know it's said: people are always cursed to live in interesting times. Critics like me were excused to an extent—nobody expected artistic judgment to be tested in combination with spooky propaganda charades. Unfortunately that was the end for me as an independent critic and curator.

I had to shun the Romanian hot potato after that, which was too bad. Caspar Velo was a clever impresario, a great party-giver, and a very entertaining fraud. (If I get a chance, I'll tell you about one of his parties later.)

"Steven James…" came the voice of Count Vlad—Velo could do others. "I have some images I vant to show you."

"Caspar, you rotten apple—I can't talk. On a crucial deadline."

"Come on, man," Velo said, but he was no longer Count Vlad; he had almost been a friend. "For old times' sake--I've got something really interesting, Steve. You'll find this--irresistible."

"OK—but I'll really have get back to you."

"This can hardly wait, you foolish man."

"Two days," I told Velo, turning back to Gail's job.

—

3.

Gail Peebles stood at a lectern in the lobby of the Emperor Rashid Nine Hotel in Dubai. She had sold the Rashid an immense Scully, at about $240k, to center the swirling sandstone wall area between their twin 65-storey tower express lifts. The Scully was a big, beautiful 20' red square, with a grey pinstripe running diagonally beneath the upper right hand corner. Gorgeous—sober and daring at the same instant; if you know what I mean.

Outside the sun was merciless. It was 120 degrees F. Jaguars and Bentleys with tinted windowpanes moved up and down the Beach Boulevard, some recklessly, others at a professionally measured pace. You could see guest-workers, like fleas scurrying over Gargantuan pumps and earth movers as they went on raising man-made islands in the Bay of Dubai which Madonna and David Beckham and others as famously rich promised to purchase. There they would construct palatial homes.

"Now, I wanna talk to you'all about Jackson Pollock," Gail drawled. She looked out over the room of multi-millionaire sheiks. "That man was all cowboy."

My Jackson Pollock reference in Gail's talk script -- "Modern art is useless for a dictator's prop" -- somebody once commented about abstract expressionism—emerged from Henry Constance's propaganda shop amplified, with a freewheeling thrust. They played up the self-reliant spirit of Pollock, tormented Montana artist, with his characteristics common to a nation of independents and entrepreneurs.

Gail could do that!

Jewelry rattled boisterously when she jabbed her finger into the air, telling Pollock's tale along with the story of 20th century, energy-plentiful Texas. Individual initiative and expression ought to know no bounds and paradise was nearly right here on Earth. Gail sure could sell it to those Arabian oil exporters, whose lifestyles negotiated cultivated restrictions.

Later in the talk, she got down to brass tacks.

"A program set up by the US Chamber of Commerce Overseas Branch will send eight outstanding students from the Emirates to London School of Economics annually, as part of an international group of 64 scholars earning an honors MBA in finance," she told the audience.

"You'all please take a look at these hand-outs or our website, after we're done. You can fund that program, Royal Scholars, and send your best and brightest to London by contributing to the listed groups that will support it.

"By god, it's great to be back in Dubai! Thanks gentlemen."

4.

Caspar Velo had another important artist in hand now, sure to be worth upwards of ten million dollars in sales. What else?

The recently deceased discovery was a Palestinian painter who did most of his best work during the 1940's,

—

and precious few had ever seen any of his stuff. But, Velo claimed, this guy had been well received by all of Jerusalem in his day. There was the hook—a uniting Mideast figure when it was still possible to imagine such.

"Nuri Said was without any doubt the first cubist painter in all of Arabia," Caspar told me. "His work follows Juan Gris. I know I can sell it, man."

"Fine," I said, "I'll come look. I'm done with Gail's work."

"Working for Gail Peebles, were you?"

"Actually, I did the work in conjunction with the US Chamber of Commerce, Overseas Cultural Branch. You know, talk scripts for one of Gail's enterprise holidays…"

"So you collaborated with Henry Constance?"

"You're right. He's fiendishly efficient."

"So I've heard," said Caspar. "So I've heard."

"What's the rush, Caspar?" With his Palestinian, I meant.

"Come on, you foolish man," he said. "You know I have to be a very good boy for the rest of my life, forever more, after the Glasnost issue. I will never be able to stop doing good."

"This is your Mideast peace initiative?"

"Absolutely and exactly. Naturally, I raise money."

"Money—what is that? What would you do with money?"

"Come *on,* you foolish man: of course money. You raise money and make money and give some to the right people."

"And make more money? I guess I wouldn't know about such stuff," I answered.

5.

Naturally money soon did begin to come, pouring into the bank accounts of several groups Gail's talks endorsed. Not every petrodollar would send bright and beautiful Arabian grad students to the LSE, however. Some portion would go to cultivate informers on Islamic extremism and to infiltrate Al-Qaeda in Iraq, via Delta Corporation of Bahrain. Etc. Henry Constance had a way of taking care of that. I think you get the drift.

6.

Caspar Velo had called it right about Nuri Said. Work was moving out nicely at pumped up prices, fueled in part by good intentions. But buying and selling artwork had always been a good way to clean up money for other sectors of the marketplace Caspar dealt with, people who wouldn't willingly contribute to any just cause. In line with agreements he had made when he was allowed to slip through the nets after the Glasnost scam, Caspar was making sure a percentage of the proceeds from these Nuri Said transactions proceeded to the right people--people who would work against Islamic terrorism wherever its ugly mug might appear. He *was* doing that, wasn't he?

You could hardly ever be sure.

7.

I didn't often get a call from a sheik. Ali Abu Yas wanted to talk about something he had bought for his Palace Yas Dubai All Suite Hotel.

"Steven, the matter I want to talk over with you is a bit delicate…"

"Go ahead, sir, please."

"I've become a little uncertain about our new Nuri Said piece, you see. How can I be perfectly sure that it's genuine? And I hate to say this—even if it is, I'm kicking myself because I know we paid far too much for it."

"Who sold it to you, sir?"

"Gail Peebles, of course."

For a few seconds, I said nothing, then, "Well, you must trust her to verify your piece. As for price, she should be somewhere around the fair valuation…"

"Yes, I suppose. It's only that—you see, in the context of her fundraisers, I'm afraid all of us here can find ourselves…carried away."

"I understand…" I knew this man could dispose of vast resources, and that whatever was carried away from him would be carried back shortly. I was loathe to tell him that I had created some of the brochure copy.

"Steven, allow me to ask you this: is it possible that Gail wouldn't herself know if a piece were false?"

"Not likely, but not impossible," I told him. "Can I have a look at it after you talk to…?"

"I'll fly you over here if need be."

"Probably not necessary. I'll make a few calls. Back to you by the end of business today sir."

8.

I was afraid of what I might find out. I was afraid to learn that Nuri Said might be nothing but another manufactured fraud. That Caspar had once more set up an adept and bogus factory to turn out attractive phonies with a cloaked pedigree. That Gail had bought one of them to please her client. That again, it was all trumped up, a theatrical intersection of different Grand Theft schemes, one canceling another. A lot of money would go up in smoke and quite a few Arabian gentlemen were going to be understandably pissed.

9.

I began making calls, hoping I was wrong. Then an e-mail from Gail Peebles popped up. She was mad with the fire and fury of hell, wondering why some of the money for

—

her groups hadn't been deposited into the numbered accounts where it was supposed to go. She obviously needed someone to blame—whoever came readily to hand.

'What would I possibly have to do with that?' I shot an e-mail back.

The phone rang and Gail came on.

"In the name of God what are you doin' with Ali Abu Yas, Steven? None of that is any of your business! That's my client!"

"None of what? The gentleman called me, Gail. I'm a consultant--you know--I do things for people who ask me to help them. You, for example."

"Well, I don't know Steven," Gail crackled. "…Anybody can be a consultant."

"I suppose so…and you don't know what?"

"I don't know if I'll be asking for your help again…"

I said nothing.

"Oh, God, I gotta go!" She cried out like a coed in Hawaii with a make-up problem and her date already on the doorstep of the Tiki hut.

"I need to be talking to Henry Constance, not wasting my precious time with you, sucker. Good-bye!"

She crashed the receiver down, making my eardrum feel like a single dollar in free fall against the Euro. And since I never seemed to know better than to help people out with their evil deeds, it seemed possible that, in fact, my currency might devalue.

10.

I had called it correctly this time, never mind that that has not made me rich as of yet. But I am still afloat. I have a strong feeling that Gail won't be working with Henry Constance in the Mideast anymore. When it came to Caspar—well, you couldn't find him.

Months later, I was congratulating Elizabeth at the inauguration of her brand-new, spacious Gallery E. She looked the perfect near-six-foot blonde, carrying not an extra ounce of any variety of fat, and dolled up in a pink 50's business dress suit and catty black framed specs, madly ravishing and maddeningly out-of-reach, as women twenty-five years younger than this bloody old man tend to.

I couldn't be blamed for bringing up Gail Peebles.

"It's sincerely and seriously too bad," Elizabeth commiserated, breaking out of the grand-opening party mood for a moment with me. "If Gail can't sell any more artwork in the Emirates, you can see what kind of big loss that will be for the international community."

"A shame," I said to Elizabeth. "A real shame."

"Yes, Steven—yes. Oh—look who's over there!" Arms akimbo, Elizabeth fluttered off.

—

Then I went out past the wine and cheese table into the tropical District of Columbia darkness, and hopped into my car to head home quickly. I was hoping to find my wife still awake. We might have a party, even if it wouldn't be like one of Caspar Velo's.

—

Any News Is Good

1.

A shot rang out in front of the new Hotel M. Rio de Janeiro at nine p.m. last Monday evening. Two women screamed. Mrs. Mary Keeley, a delegate to the travel convention from Louisville, slumped to the ground. From inside the mirrored lobby, I thought I could see a photographer's flash snap. Then the automatic doors slid open, and a porter stood over the lifeless heap.

I turned quickly on my heels and took the elevator up. Inside the car, women were combing out their reflections while the indicator fluttered from one to three. I forced my way to the front and stepped out, figuring that the hotel's having rolled out the red carpet might be a good way into my lead.

Amy Bensten was alone in the press suite. She was straining over her typewriter, updating a promotional release.

"Hey," she looked startled as I came up behind her. "How about giving me a hand with this?"

"Better forget it," I said. "A woman's just been shot downstairs."

"You're crazy," Amy glanced over the release. "It couldn't happen here, we've just opened the damn place."

"I'm telling you what I just saw. Now clear that hype off the typewriter and go look for yourself, if you want a real story."

Amy was stubborn. She sat there, fingering the upper case key. Just then there was a flurry of activity out in the hall. Pierre Martinez, the chain's publicity agent, came whirling into the room, long arms and legs flapping like signal flags before a dawn raid. He saw me and stopped.

"Amy, get downstairs, quick." Martinez tugged on the back of her chair.

"Don't tell me..."

Martincz was already annoyed. He took a step backward and pointed a thin finger. "Listen, get down to the lobby. A woman's been shot...We'll have to come up with a story."

Amy looked confused, but she knew what side her bread was buttered on. She got up and went out of the press room.

"Did you see it?" Martinez turned to me.

"I heard it. I was in the lobby when she was shot. Have they picked up anyone?"

"There's a suspect. The police are questioning him in Deacon's office."

Right here at the hotel?"

"Deacon is arranging everything. We'll have to work closely with the police, 'til we can get the story straightened out."

"Look, Martinez, it doesn't sound good to me. I don't see how you're going to keep the lid on this."

—

Martinez brushed me off. With a note of contempt reserved for those meddling with his arrangements, he said, "Remember, at the moment you are here working for us. The travel convention. .. the hotel is what matters. You're not working for your newspaper. Do everybody a favor and help Amy in the lobby... just get out of my way."

I stood facing my temporary superior with my hands on my hips, quietly crumpling a few notes I had made, "I don't think I like this kind of publicity campaign, Martinez. I don't like it."

He cut me off quickly, "Then you can quit and walk out. Go back to your newspaper and tell them you didn't like covering the Hotel M." Martinez laughed, savoring the fact that he had me. "Otherwise, see what you can find out and be at Deacon's office in about an hour. Clear?"

I sneered and stalked out of the room, grimacing as I hurried down the cinder-blocked flight of fire stairs to the mezzanine. Travel conventioneers were gathered in clusters below me in the hotel lobby. They looked like a pack of cards being broken in for an all-night game. Near the door, a porter was cleaning blood spots off the rug. To my left was a lady wearing a name tag, Her name wag Sturges, something Sturges.

"Did you see what happened?" I asked.

"I don't know...they say one of our attendees was shot downstairs, isn't that right, Frank?" She tugged on the sleeve of a burly man 1 took to be her husband.

"Yeah, that's right. And who the hell are you, anyway?" Frank pointed a fat finger at the spot where my convention credentials should have been pinned.

I reached into my back pocket for the blue billfold where I normally kept my press card.

Frank Sturges stepped back and said, "What cha lookin' for son?"

"My press card. I work for the local paper."

"Reporter, eh?" said Frank, tugging his wife away. "Why didn't you tell us in the first place?"

"Look--I'm working for the hotel during convention week. We have to get out a story..." I let that trail off as Frank Sturges and his wife moved away. Instead I glided down the escalator to the lobby, where Amy was desperately pumping the porter for information.

"What was she wearing?"

"Who?" said the porter, wiping the last fleck of soap suds off the damp tile.

"Mrs. Keeley..."

"I don't remember Ms., I'm sorry."

"Are you sure?"

"I already told you," the man said, "I didn't see nothin! The ambulance took her right away."

The porter looked at me sideways as I passed him, stepped on the grooved rubber floor mat, and walked out through the automatic door. Apart from the few extra cops who watched doormen helping people in and of cabs, there was nothing in front of the hotel to indicate that a fatal shooting had occurred there half an hour before.

—

I lit a cigarette and went over to talk to Dick Farney, our photographer.

"Were you out here when it happened?" I asked.

"Sure," said Farney, "Looks like I was the only photographer on the scene."

I frowned, "When are you going to develop the film?"

"Along with the batch I'm taking back to the paper."

"You're not going sooner?"

"Martinez told me not to worry about it, just to come back when the batch was done."

"And that's all he said?"

Farney said, "Right...what's your problem?"

"I don't know what the hell I'm doing around here, the way Martinez handles things."

"Maybe you're right. But we're not working for the paper now, but for him," Farney said. He struck an insolent pose against as expensive sedan. "He'll probably put the whole story together for us. But they gotta have me around for their dammed pictures."

Farney patted the black camera bag which hung down against his hip.

I said, "Doesn't do me much good..."

I shrugged my shoulders and strode off in the direction of the ocean. Crossing the seafront avenue, I saw the Hotel M. looming like a huge black mirror. The waves were spraying whips of water over the sand. I sat down, turned to look at the hotel through the mist, and spent half an hour staring into the surf trying to forget the whole thing.

When I turned around again and to go, I was a little surprised to see the hotel still standing out, contemporary grey against the mountains and the moonlit sky.

"Disappear," I took a handful of sand and flung it into the wind. It blew back into my face. Down the beach the tide was coming up above the level where I was standing. It was time to attend the meeting in Deacon's office.

2.

Amy Bensten was nowhere as I reached the mezzanine. Below, the pack of convention delegates had shuffled into some new order, but there didn't seem to be meaning in the change. Frank Sturges and his wife were located at the other end of the check-in counter, just ten feet from where they stood half an hour before.

"Nice night," I said to Frank Sturges as I passed him on the way to the elevators. He wheeled around and caught himself starting to agree.

Martinez and Amy were talking with Deacon in the director's office when I came in. Martinez sat, carefully arranging the collar of his dress shirt. Deacon, the half-Frenchman from New Orleans, motioned for me to sit, holding his glasses up to the light with his other hand. He wore ruffled cuffs with his black suit.

—

"Ready with a story?" I asked Amy in workaday fashion.

She looked offended and said nothing.

"It appears that Mrs. Keeley arranged to have herself killed," Martinez spoke up quickly, playing with a hotel pen set that pointed upward from the Formica topped table.

Deacon watched me through the top half of his bifocals.

"How do you figure..?" I asked. "Do you expect me to write that? To buy you a quiet evening?"

"You can try talking to the police, but they won't tell you a thing right now. You'd be wasting your time." Martinez spoke with the weariness of those to whom everything is perfectly clear. They wonder why people don't see it the same way.

"Listen Robbins, Amy's going to take care of the story. Don't worry yourself," he said to me.

"Why don't you just forget it until morning?" Deacon said apologetically.

"Seems this woman was trying to prove some point. We can't have it spoil everything we're trying to accomplish."

"Who's the killer?" I turned again to Amy. "Come on guys..."

Without looking up from the set of notes she had scribbled on her pad, Amy said, "They're holding an American from the convention."

"I hardly believe a word of this," I said, getting up quickly out of my chair.

"Who is this guy? And what's his connection to Mrs. Keeley?"

Nothing was said, no one moved.

"OK. I'll sit on it until the morning, like you say." I started out of the room.

"Listen," Martinez spoke up like a knife in the back, "If you see Farney out front, remind him to get here with the photos tomorrow, asap."

"Right, boss." I hustled down the fire stairs, hot under the collar. When I got to the front entrance, the doorman told me that Farney had left a few minutes before. I gazed back into the lobby for a moment, then hailed a taxi.

We sped along the highway, between the line of high rise concrete soldiers and the yachts bobbing in the bay. I hated Martinez's way of handling things, but was it worth the trouble to meddle in his business?

'Let Amy take care of it.' Sure.

My taxi pulled up to the newspaper building. At two a.m. there was nothing on the poorly lit street except a few hookers, and the men tottering to and fro with them to tawdry hotels. I opened the big blue door at the paper, then walked up two flights to the darkroom.

From behind several folds of black drapes Farney called for me to wait a minute.

—

Then he opened up, admitting me to his little sanctum, awash in red light.

"Here they are." Farney pointed to a grey plastic basin. About twenty prints were floating face down.

"Are they ready?" I asked him, in the tone of an initiate to the mysteries of developing film.

"Yeah, you can look in a minute." Farney moved around adroitly in the bloodshot darkness, checking a list on the opposite worktable. I saw his pencil poised.

"Can't see how you can even read your list in here...Oh, by the way, who's that young lady that's been working up here during the last few days?"

Farney ignored me. "Turn the prints over now if you want a look...they should be ready," he said. He kept studying his list, looking away from me.

I started sliding the photos over one by one, keeping the entire batch in the wet tray. They had a funny way of bending one over the other, swaying in the solution like paper seaweed. One hadn't come out well and would have to be thrown out. I saw something I didn't like.

"What happened with this one?" I asked Farney, pulling the blurred shot out of the developing bath.

He squinted in the red light, saying "Which is it?"

"It's the one where the victim looks like she's standing in front of the doors, waiting to go in. Must have been the moment before she was shot." I held the blurred photo up.

"Oh, that one," Farney said carelessly, coming over to look at other photos. "It didn't turn out well. It's underexposed."

"Can you get a better print?" I was looking over his shoulder at other shots of the hotel taken from the front. The doors were open, framing the porter's twisted face as he watched a pair of grim attendants put Mrs. Keeley's body on a stretcher. Then I held the ruined print over my head and began moving it around under the dim red light. There was a dark mass with a lighter glint. The highlighted doorway framed Mrs. Keeley as an upright smudge. She seemed to be adjusting a hat on her head. One spindly raised arm was the clearest thing in the picture.

"Could you make me another one of these for me, Farney?" I studied the photo for a facial expression I wanted to see. "Bring up the tones a bit?"

Farney pulled the wet batch of work out of the basin, letting it drip onto slatted floor. He said, "Look, you don't think there are enough decent shots? Enough to make up your hotel pages? Give me a break, it's near three a.m."

"Sure, Farney, fine work," I said and moved toward the door. "But I saw something interesting in that bad print."

"Wait a minute," Farney turned around. "Do not open the door like that. I've got work over here I still need to finish."

"So how do I get out?"

"Hang on, about, that photo, what cha mean?" Farney asked.

—

"I'm not sure--looks like an interesting shot--I'm curious to see the look on her face right before the shooting started."

"You should be curious." Farney didn't make a move to let me out. He said, "OK, I'll do you another, since you like it so well."

"Thanks," I said to Farney. "Now how about letting me out of this room? I need some sleep."

Farney opened the door a crack. He said, "I'll have the print for you tomorrow morning, around, ten. I'm showing them the whole batch, at the Hotel M." He hesitated, then told me to slip out quickly.

I went down the steps and to the street to look for a taxi. We pulled past whores lolling beneath the arches of Lapa, around gaping subway excavations and then I was asleep, forgetting about the damned hotel promotion and the murder of Mrs. Mary Keeley.

3.

The sea glistened in the morning sun on the other side of a hotel window cut for a vista of the sprawling beachfront. Traffic spilled wildly around the city: buses leaned above the roadway; careening sports cars threatened cafe customers with a sidewise roll into their laps.

I stood at the window, watching. It was clear that they had chosen a great spot for their hotel. They had done everything right, set it all up, considered everything. And what about Mrs. Keeley, where had she gone wrong? I couldn't find an answer out the window. The orange carpet in Martinez's office went just as deep: it would look good for the few days the average guest might spend in a room, after that, someone else would get to look.

I don't know how long I stood, just staring at the floor. Then Pierre Martinez was there: two pointed black Italian shoes on the orange carpet.

"Oh," he said. "How are you?...Have you seen Farney this morning?"

"No. He said he'd be here early...but he must have worked past three..." I turned away from Martinez to gaze at the ocean again.

"Good." Martinez seemed to like dealing with people when their backs were turned. "The meeting should be starting right now!"

"Where's Amy?" I cut him off.

"She's been talking with Deacon for the last half hour..."

"I'm on time," I said.

Martinez asked, "But you haven't seen Farney this morning?"

"Not since 2:30 a.m. What are you driving at, Martinez?"

"About the photos: did Farney show them to you?"

"No," I lied. "Farney told me they came out OK when I talked to him by phone."

"So you called him at the paper?" Martinez began drumming his fingers absently on top of a brown leather chair, then picked s spot of lint off the top corner and threw it down.

Can it be that I heard a spot of lint hit the meeting room carpet? At that — I turned around. Amy Bensten walked in, followed by Deacon, his light beige summer suit beginning to dampen. Farney came next with the black camera bag swinging under his arm. A police inspector was with them.

"Sit down everyone," said Deacon. "This is Inspector Machado from the 19th precinct, Rio."

Amy looked nervous. As she shifted into a chair, her white and orange frock picked up red from her flushing cheeks.

"We'll have coffee," Deacon told a white-jacketed porter, who quickly left the room.

Deacon, pressing his arms firmly down onto the mahogany table in front of him, asked the inspector, "Are you still holding the man in connection with Mrs. Keeley's murder?"

Inspector Machado stood up. He wore a dark blue suit with a white shirt and narrow black tie. The tie was too narrow, I thought. Machado's face looked like a hawk's; his olive brown nose protruded like a sensitive beak. He asked, "Can I see the photos that were taken in front of the hotel yesterday?"

Farney chafed as he opened his bag, rummaged around and drew three photos out. I stared at his black bag as he handed them to Inspector Machado. The bag sat on the table, like a stone.

The photos on the table were the same Farney showed me. There was the hotel, there the hotel porter, there the dead woman being taken away. What was the story? Inspector Machado picked them up one at a time.

"Any others?" he asked.

Deacon was re-doing his tie, looking misshapen despite the air-conditioning.

Martinez and Farney exchanged the look of two men in the game with ace high against a full house.

"A couple didn't turn out well," Farney started in haltingly. He looked at what was face up on the table. He appealed to Inspector Machado, "What's wrong with those? I think they're good shots don't you?"

"I was hoping for more," said Inspector Machado. "As the ambulance had already gone and the crime scene was disturbed before our forensic people arrived."

It was up to Martinez. He arranged the collar of his grey shirt with thin fingers. I expected a defense of the faith.

"Inspector, Farney is the best photographer working in Rio," Martinez explained, focusing on Machado 's discriminating beak. The nose was trained to sniff statements out of the air, shunting lies to the side, breathing pure truth deep.

"Apparently," Martinez began, "there are two more photos which haven't shown up well, Inspector. What was the problem, Farney?"

"Underexposed," said Farney.

"And you're going back to the lab with those?"

—

"Yeah, I'll do my best.."

Inspector Machado picked up three photos from the conference table, saying, "I'll give you one hour, Mr. Farney. Then I want all the film you shot yesterday, developed or not..."

Farney got to his feet quickly.

Once he had left, Machado said to the rest of us, "We're not considering the theory that Mrs. Keeler arranged her own death."

Deacon and Martinez could find nothing to say.

I left the room and found Farney in the hallway, pacing in front of the elevators. He drummed his heels on the snappy grey tiles. He caught sight of me on the drill of one mean step.

"What do you want?" Farney's voice crackled.

"You promised me a look, remember?" The doors of the elevator opened and I followed Farney into an empty car. I asked, "Where were you this morning?"

"Deacon called me in as soon as I came through the door. He wanted to talk before the cop got here."

"Martinez, was he there too?"

On the ground floor now, I said, "Let's go." I headed around a corner. The escalator lifted a couple of guests on its smooth curve.

Farney stood behind me, saying "Let's go is right." He sprang to life and brushed by me into the jostling crowd.

"I've got just one hour, you heard what he said."

I had to hustle to keep up with him. I said, "You have one hour to do what? Develop photos you already have? What about my copy?!"

"Deal's off," said Farney.

4.

The 19th precinct house roasted in the lunchtime sun. Sitting on a busy corner of Avenida Copacabana with black and purple exhaust fumes swallowing it, it looked like a very special corridor between hell and paradise. I went in.

In the grey entry hall two men sat with piles of papers on a slatted bench. The wooden bench was also painted grey. The men looked like athletes getting ready to toss piles of paper through hoops. One was pointing at the other. Opposite the warm-up bench sat the precinct call desk, set back two feet behind a retaining fence. The two officials at the desk tried to look impassive, but were nearer to oblivion and sleep.

"Got a match?" I asked one of the deputies from my side of the retainer. He didn't seem to hear, so I asked again.

"Rudin," the official called out, "Have you got a light for this foreigner?"

A man who had been sweeping the inner corridor put down his broom. He struck a match near my face. He seemed hurt when I didn't take out a cigarette. He said, "What is it, mister?"

I looked up at the indolent totem of the desk. The deputy on the left asked me, "What's your business here?".

—

"I'm a reporter." I handed my ID across the rail. Rudin held his palms face upward and proceeded back to his broom. The police deputy stared at my credentials like a cretin eyeing the Rosetta stone.

"I'm working out of the M. Hotel," I explained to the hot weather.| "During the travel convention."

The deputy allowed a telephone to ring incessantly at his elbow.

"Inspector Machado is on the third floor, room six. He pointed in the direction of the stairwell. "Keep that card in your hand."

I took the first steps with a bounce. On the landing, I noticed that the deputy had pinned a purple tag to my press credential.

There was cracked yellow paint surviving on the third floor walls like a reminder of lives pissed away. The assortment of men in the hallway fell on various sides of the law. I passed them and stared at the translucent glass door at 306, trying to fathom the shadows that shifted behind it.

Farney was in the office, staring across the desk at Inspector Machado. Spread out between them were ten or so photos. Machado stood to show me another hardwood chair. I sat down. The chair was about as comfortable as forced labor.

Machado spoke, "Mr. Farney," he began, opening his hands to take in the tabletop, "Mr. Farney has come up with another couple of photos."

His eyes flitted over the array, "In addition to those we were shown this morning...Here," Machado picked up a couple.

I tensed, waiting for him to hand them over. To my left, Farney sat impenetrably behind a pair of expensive sunglasses. Machado looked over the batch one by one before putting them on the desk. "I imagine you won't have seen these," he said to me.

There was one I hadn't seen. It clearly showed Mrs. Keeley getting out of a cab at the hotel curbside; a white jacketed porter bent to take her arm. There was someone else in the cab.

"This must have been right before the shooting occurred," I said.

Machado directed my attention back towards the photo and asked, "Do you know the other person in the taxi?"

I said I didn't.

"Well, Mr. Farney has identified him as Perry Miller, the man we are questioning now. The other photo, have you seen that?"

Farney grimaced. Across the table Machado's nasal radar flared, ready for the work of detection.

The other shot was no clearer than it had been the night before, and I told Inspector Machado, "No I haven't seen this."

"It's not easy to make out, is it?" Machado was studying one copy. "Farney says it won't be easy to get a better print..."

"I've tried twice," Farney spoke up. "I'll try once more, Inspector."

—

"Do that, Mr. Farney." The police inspector leaned over to press a buzzer at the side of his desk. A wiry guy wearing a Brazil soccer jersey came from the hall. "Go get him," Machado told the man, motioning towards the door.

When Farney started to follow the deputy into the corridor Machado held up a hand like a traffic cop, "One minute," his hawk's beak twitched. "You needn't be in such a hurry."

The skinny deputy pushed a tall American into the room, and left. The man wore a blue and white checked short sleeved shirt and was handcuffed. He chafed like a home run king during the off season.

"Sit down Miller." Machado motioned toward a flat bench.

"You may know photographer Dick Farney." Machado tipped his head to address Miller. "This is another gentleman of the American press, Mr. Robbins."

Perry Miller was a travel agent. He glanced from his bound hands to Farney.

"Miller has admitted to firing the gun which killed Mrs. Keeler," Inspector Machado said abruptly. "But he swears he was told the gun would be loaded with blanks. In fact, Mr. Miller was a friend of the deceased..."

"Who put you up to it?" I asked Miller.

Inspector Machado answered for him, "His instructions came from Pierre Martinez of the Hotel M...who was apparently working with Mrs. Keeley,"

I stammered, "And Martinez, what does he have to say about it? Does he go running free?"

"No, no," Machado breathed in deeply. "He's confined to the hotel. He admits to his part in the scheme, They were interested in a publicity photo which would show the woman safe the hotel lobby after the shot rang out. Of course, it had to appear within the context of..." Machado hesitated, sniffing.

"The real news," I said cynically to Farney. "Your specialty...indirect publicity."

Machado had recovered his air supply. "That's what it's known as. But Martinez also denies anything involving a loaded weapon. They were going to report an attempted murder, Mrs. Keeley would drop the charges and Miller would fly home--perhaps a few days late. Any news is good—don't they say?"

"What does Deacon think?"

"Could they carry out the operation without Deacon knowing?" Machado asked Farney. "Deacon says the whole thing was in Martinez's hands."

"That's probably true," Farney said.

"And Amy Bensten, what does she know?"

"Come on," Farney said.

Inspector Machado held his palms face up like scales of justice. He said, "Nothing much, Robbins. We assume she knows very little. Do you have questions for Mr. Miller?"

Either the handcuffs or his suntan must have been weighing Miller down.

"What about it, Miller?"

—

"To tell the truth, I fired the gun, so what's the use?"

"But you wouldn't be guilty if what you say is true...if you'd been told you'd be firing blanks. The man who crossed you would be."

Machado faced me squarely from his desk. He said, "Robbins, we've been through this with Mr. Miller."

"I can't imagine why anyone would have wanted Mrs. Keeley killed," said Miller.

"And what about Martinez, who put him up to it?"

"Come on," said Farney. I was wasting his time it appeared. "It's hard to see what Martinez would have to gain."

Machado said, "We know that Martinez has been fighting very hard to retain his position with the hotel chain. Several executives are trying to recall him after the shooting incident."

I turned to Miller, and asked, "Are you sure Martinez didn't have any other connection with Mrs. Keeley? At one point Deacon said she'd arranged to have herself done in...how do you figure that?"

"I don't know," Miller shrugged, "It might be something they'd say to stall or make it easier on me."

Inspector Machado said, "I think Miller's had enough for today." He leaned sleepily back in his chair.

"Just a couple of more questions?" I wanted to keep his hand off the buzzer.

Machado frowned. "All right." He turned to Farney, "Take these back to your lab...I'll see you back here within a couple of hours."

Farney scooped up one copy of each printed photo from the pile on the inspector's desk. Brushing by Miller, he went out of the room without stopping to put the photos into his black bag.

I waited while the sound of Farney's footsteps was lost in the hall. I addressed Miller, "Can you tell me more about Mrs. Keeley's affiliation...did she have had any special connection to the Hotel M?"

"She worked for Star Tours, a Louisville Agency." Miller said.

"Could Mrs. Keeley's agency have threatened to direct their clients elsewhere? In which case Martinez might have had some beef with her."

" I don't know of any problems between Hotel M. and Star. Death would be a crazy revenge."

Machado roused himself. "Where is this taking us, Robbins?"

"I'm almost done, Inspector."

Machado pressed the buzzer under his desk.

I decided to get what I could. Lifting Farney's underexposed print from the inspector's desk I said, "Where do you know Mrs. Keeley from, Miller? You're from New York, aren't you?"

—

"That's right. I work for Worldwide Tours on Fifth Avenue. I met Mrs. Keeley on a flight to Los Angeles four or five years ago. There was another travel trade promotion show."

"You both took part?"

"Mary Keeley and I were judges of photography."

Machado nodded and pushed his button.

On the tabletop the photo copies seemed to swim in a kind of motion, which might never quite tell the story.

"Go ahead," Machado said as the deputy took Miller's arm to lead him out.

I brushed by Miller and his unhealthy warden in the foul yellow hallway. A moment later I emerged from the stifling precinct house into brilliant afternoon sunshine.

5.

Back at the paper I met no one on the way to the darkroom. Pressed tightly against the dark crepe, I strained to hear the sounds of water swishing in grey basins. Someone was night fishing in red light; the wooden floorboards creaked. The door held fast when I pushed.

"Just a minute, I'm coming out," Farney's voice came before the latch popped. He looked surprised to see me.

"Hello, Dick," I said. "Can I take a look?"

"Sure, just a sec." Farney pushed past me and moved toward a small hallway bathroom. He closed the door halfway. He asked, "Did you stay at the precinct long?"

"No it took time to get here during rush hour."

"Oh yeah? Did you learn anything from Miller?" Farney said.

"Nothing. I can't see just what would be in it for him."

"A payoff, maybe?" Water was running in the sink. "A lousy rotten payoff." Farney opened the bathroom door and stood lazily against its frame, checking his watch.

I said, "This has been difficult...I don't remember having a day as tough as this, even back in the states."

Farney nodded, assenting as he cupped palms to light his cigarette.

"I asked Farney, Where did you work?"

"In New York, for a while. But mostly L.A., that's where I'm from. I've worked all over California."

"So you worked for an L.A. paper?"

Farney shrugged. "Some of the time...but I did other gigs...magazines, publicity for films, travel promotions..."

"You must have been doing very well..." I said.

"Well? In fact I was taking off."

"What about that travel promotion show, then?" I made a stab.

—

Farney's cigarette had burned down halfway. He threw it to the floor and ground it out. He said, "What's that?"

"You know what I'm talking about, Farney. The show Miller and Mrs. Keeley attended in LA. Where they were judges?"

He took half a step in my direction, "What about it? Blind judges who robbed me of a prize I deserved! I had so many wonderful shots. They didn't get my style."

I braced myself in front of the black drape, balancing on the balls of my feet. Enraged, Farney leapt at me, knocking me backward through the black hanging, into the darkroom. The door opened, then snapped back on its hinge, catching Farney on the side of his head. He wobbled like a drunken sailor, collapsing against a workbench. I hit the wall switch, flickering on the fluorescent lights, then dunked my hand into the grey plastic bath.

Five photos came up dripping and yellowing to ruin under the light. Mrs. Keeley posed in one of then, with a small black hat and a look which read pure terror.

I moved my thumb; the face washed blank, but I realized she had recognized Dick Farney.

6.

The sun made a rosy setting behind the green hump of Corcovado, giving the surviving travel conventioneers and others who had the time to look a late afternoon treat. Atop the hill Christ the Redeemer shed divine mercy along with the day's last rays of natural light upon the homebound.

My taxi headed along the shoreline highway towards the hotel, and the end of another job.

Pierre Martinez was talking on a red telephone when I went through his office door at the M. By the time I reached his neatly arranged desk he had promised to call the party right back. He hung up the phone with an irate click, folded his arms and did not ask me to leave.

"What's going to happen to Miller?" I rested my palms on the Formica desk top, thrusting my chin forward.

Martinez did not hurry. ""Why don't you take a load off your feet?" he offered.

"That's kind of you," I said. "Now, are we going to allow Miller to spend a few years in a Brazilian jail?" I remained on my feet and kept my eyes on Martinez and the orange shag carpet, feeling about as comfortable as a man on an uncharted minefield.

"What makes you want to get so wrapped up in this?" Martinez moved a finger to fix his shirt.

"I want you to admit how much you knew." I leant downward on my palms.

"...How about a straight answer?"

"About what?" Martinez wanted to know. The bay window behind his back showed off the blue sea, pure and simple.

"Why did you frame Miller?"

"And why should I repeat to you what I've already discussed with Inspector Machado?" Martinez shot back,

—

his polished nails clasping a cigarette. "I had no idea that the gun would be loaded..."

"Seriously? At no time? You never saw Farney handle the gun?"

Gloom spread grey spots on his face.

I pulled a manila envelope from my inside pocket and took out the photo Farney had been unable to improve upon. Martinez stared at it, his face going to a chalky blank. He ground his unlit cigarette into a silver ashtray and picked up the photo with two unsteady hands.

"Why show me this?" he said shrilly. He handed the photo back. "I can't see anything here." The sea unfurled smoothly beyond Martinez's picture window. It looked like a nice beach day.

"Take a careful look," I sat down on the edge of his desk.

"What do you want?" Martinez asked.

"I want you to see what your stinking little promo scheme comes to, Martinez. Imagine: Telling me that she wanted to be killed!"

"OK--That was our first thought. Mrs. Keeley had agreed to set herself up for a phony murder..." He stopped himself from going on too smoothly. "It seemed plausible."

"Now we know better. Come on Martinez, what's your story now?"

Martinez fiddled with the cigarette butt, arranging a pattern.

"Enough!" I pointed my finger at the photographic target. "The police are going to conclude you're also responsible soon...Farney's out cold in the photo lab...They'll figure that you knew the gun wasn't loaded with blanks. Are you going to let Miller take the rap?"

Martinez looked into my face. He must have seen the Grand Inquisitor hovering, ready with the smoking hot firebrand of Justice. He was ready to surrender!

Then his red telephone rang. Martinez crumpled into his office chair with the receiver. I heard him confirm an item with Inspector Machado. His eyes rolled like slot machine totems ringing up a million bucks.

"They'll put Miller on a plane," he said, as if in a trance. "I have to make his reservation." He began grappling spasmodically with his address book.

"You cut a deal with Machado!"

"Go: tell them about Farney...go ahead," Martinez said. "It wouldn't matter. They already know."

Carrying his rumpled intentions, he exited his office by a side door. He didn't look back.

—

WITCHES' COFFEE

A Miracle Brew from Brazil

Novella

—

WITCHES' COFFEE

A Miracle Brew from Brazil

Who's prepared to pay the price for a trip to Paradise?

Love for Sale

Prologue: A Very Brief Film

It is December, a hundred-degree day in Brazil. Two barefooted boys kick a soccer ball along damp strip of Rio de Janeiro's Flamengo Beach. Off target, a shot goes into shallow water.

One boy wades in for the ball. A small package rides in on a wave and floats near the soccer ball.

"Grab that too! Bring it here!"

The box has been wrapped in cellophane, but it is waterlogged.

"Open it!"

"No—way. Voce! You open it."

Inside the box everything is soaked. There are tangled, bright-colored ribbons, a small clay doll, an aluminum cup, and the remains of a bar of toilet soap. You can just about make out the label on the plastic soap package, *The Dream of Nymphs.*

"Look, there's a note."

The note is inside a small plastic bag. Nevertheless, the ink is smudged.

The boys read what they can:

"...a terrible secret....so ashamed...I beg you, grant..."

Silvia d....

One boy shudders.

"None of that witchcraft business," the other says. In a hurry, fearful of dark forces, they replace the lid of the waterlogged box. They throw all of it back into the unconcerned sea.

The soccer ball sits on the sand. There is not much of a breeze.

1.

"I'm a bloody fool," Vanessa Saxe muttered. "I could have married Alvaro Fontes."

She had already cried over the fact more than once during the three months since the breakup, although she was not the crying kind. 'Let's wait until the workday is done to weep, mate,' she encouraged herself.

Alvaro Fontes was a fantastic person for Vanessa, a tanned and handsome surfer, from Rio's cultured set, at 33, a partner in his family's top shelf ad agency. He had a Mercedes and a great two-handed backhand. Best of all, he

—

was a dazzling and delectable Brazilian man. How could she have gone off to 'talk over her engagement just one more time' the night before the ring-giving party—and with Hilton Folkes of all people. Hadn't she talked about it with one and all, thought it over quite enough? If you went anywhere with Hilton, nothing was certain but that you would finish with a monstrous hangover the next morning. What controlled that so-called decision to go for drinks that evening, she wondered—just what rough magic had overtaken her?

At least she had been able to summon the presence of mind to telephone and let Alvaro's family know she'd be late for the afternoon ring party. But it was no use: 'forget about showing up,' they told her flatly. In Brazil such ceremonies were the only appointments you couldn't arrive late for. All the old aunties and cousins had lined up to meet Alvaro's 'gorgeous and talented red-head from England.' Now the Fontes family of Rio de Janeiro already had a particular Carioca starlet in mind for Alvaro, since Vanessa, who was twenty-nine, didn't seem to think that arriving on time for blessed events was very important.

'She must have some serious problems!' said the aunts.

'The devil with my bloody vacillation,' Vanessa thought. 'Why couldn't I have been clear where my own life was concerned?'

That was back in September. Now Christmas was three weeks off and Vanessa did not have anyone to buy gifts for. It never snowed in Rio de Janeiro. There wasn't going to be a hearth and husband, not even a cozy date, not this time around.

Six years before, she'd wasted no time leaving England to travel after a London car crash claimed both of her parents' lives. Amazed by the beauty, and with luck at finding a job in less than a week, she had settled in Brazil.

She wondered whether she would ever see her younger sister again, without going back to visit England. She hadn't gone back. She didn't want to visit her parents' grave, since at their funeral, she had nearly gone mad. She had shamed herself with the entire Saxe family. Since she and her sister rarely talked. Vanessa was alone and lonely.

'You've done it again! You're a regular horse's arse, mate,' she thought.

It was just about four according to the hallway clock on Friday afternoon at Bright and Peters, the multinational auditing firm where Vanessa served as Chief Recruiter for Human Resources. Her stay away from England, living in Rio de Janeiro had been four sun-splashed and seemingly successful years leading toward a perfect marriage with Alvaro Fontes. But now?

A strong swimmer and tennis player, Vanessa had usually been able to persuade herself that she was an Olympian, and she had plenty of opportunity to develop the role, as she looked both fresh cream appetizing and perfectly fit alongside the uniformly bronzed, homegrown Brazilian gods and goddesses. She could also look down her nose fiercely, when necessary, to the dismay of unsuspecting ordinary souls who had the nerve to believe they could be effective messenger boys, receptionists, or doormen. At High and Peters the red-haired hatchet woman from Personnel was piously feared.

Except that now, sitting at her desk, she was trying not to cry.

—

Four years in Brazil…Vanessa's progression from recent college graduate to world wanderer to corporate manager had been notoriously swift. There had been a defining moment: Teaching English after she'd decided to stay awhile in Rio, Vanessa had tasted it neat. Tuesdays and Thursdays, she traveled on the streetcar up the hillside to Santa Theresa district, where she taught English to a private pupil, Dr. Mariano de Abreu, an elderly Brazilian shareholder in a multinational pharmaceutical firm. The family's triplex concrete mansion overhung a green forest and red-brown soil Santa Teresa slope: in every direction trembling houses held onto the hillsides. Stepping off the streetcar at the Abreu's entrance gate, Vanessa saw a medieval compound, fortified against the masses, the magic and the misery of Brazil. When dinner ended, a white-jacketed, white-gloved butler would brush the de Abreu food crumbs from the table into a little silver dustpan.

Vanessa next taught the old gentleman in the sedate living room, later riding an elevator between levels of the cantilever-constructed mansion to give a class to Dr. Mariano's dark haired and languid daughter, Claudia, in her study adorned with the poster of Roberto Carlos.

Opulence! Oligarchy! Royalty? Yes!

'Come on mate,' Vanessa now admonished herself, 'let's check those emotions: it's Friday afternoon and there are places to go.'

Her office telephone rang. The moments of reflection would have to cease. They were sending someone up to see her.

Vanessa glanced at her desktop calendar. 'How could this Dr. Roderigo de Moraes be visiting my office at such a god-forsaken moment?' she wondered. 'Who made this appointment?' Then she went into the corridor to wait for the man.

'At least he doesn't look too bad,' she consoled herself as the doctor left the elevator. She watched professionally as he walked in her direction, following a white-jacketed porter. On a closer look, she noticed that he might have been composed with a touch of the old tar brush, was that a tiny droplet of African ink...as people in her international group might say.

They shook hands in the corporate hallway.

"You're here for our interview then, doctor?"

"Yes—Ms. Saxe?"

Dr. Roderigo gave the tall, tanned over pink-skinned redhead the once-over. She was different from a Brazilian gal, of course. He took out a little rag and polished his tortoise shell spectacles in an instant.

"Pardon me, Ms. Saxe," he said.

"It's awfully late on Friday, but let's go in..."

In the office, she looked down at her desktop again. Yes, this must be the consulting psychiatrist candidate. Vanessa remembered making notes on his file a few days before; he would be a shade shy of forty. They sat.

Bright and Peters was located on the top floor of a twenty story-tower in downtown Rio. The windows behind

Vanessa, beyond her flaming red mane, gave Dr. Roderigo a wide-angle view of Guanabara Bay, including Sugar Loaf, where cable cars were moving up and down, just as they

—

had when Jaws tried to sink his metallic fangs into James Bond. The brown mass of the mountain thrust up there, towering above the choppy waves of the bay.

"Voce tem uma vista muito boa," said Dr. Roderigo de Moraes.

"Rio *is* the marvelous city, and this is a great office with an exceptional view." Vanessa admitted. "Cidade Maravilhosa, Marvelous indeed, as you Brazilians claim. Are you from here, a Carioca, Doctor Roderigo?"

"No, I come from Minas state."

Check mark--that region produced many of the most industrious Brazilians, she had come to believe. The Rio people were better for parties. Lanky Vanessa had been invited to quite a few.

There was an instant of silence.

"So your family migrated to Rio at some point?"

"No, not all of us, Ms. Saxe. I came here to attend university. I came alone, that is, I first stayed with relatives..."

Something went slack inside, and Vanessa could not help herself. 'Just too much of a bother,' she thought, and knew she felt no determination to interview a job applicant at the moment. Such a lack of concentration was practically unknown to Vanessa at the office, but someplace inside of her, Alvaro Fontes continued to foment an inconvenient rebellion.

"I'm sorry, Vanessa," Alvaro had said to her soon after the engagement was called off. "You don't do this to your family in Brazil."

"Come on, Alvaro, you and I—together we've drunk plenty....and not been able to get up on a weekend morning!"

"Was I supposed to tell that to my Mother?" he interrupted. He gave the coup de grace, "I'm sorry that you are alone in the world, Vanessa. Now I guess it will stay that way for some time."

"Doctor Roderigo, I have to be direct with you," she said flatly, in the midst of re-composing herself. "I can hardly see launching into a full interview now. We'd be working together often if the company decides to sign you on, and yes, I will need to know you well. We will have to spend time. But frankly," she stood up from her chair and continued restlessly, "At the moment I'm anxious to get out of town for the weekend."

"Anxious?" asked Dr. Roderigo. "Is something wrong?"

"Oh, that was just a figure of speech, I suppose." She paused, measuring the Brazilian and said, "To be honest, doctor, I *am* a little upset this afternoon."

"May I ask you why, Ms. Saxe?"

Vanessa did not struggle with the temptation to confess to this affable Minas Gerais psychiatrist. She said, "Oh, you know how it can be with young ladies. Man troubles."

"I hope it's not too serious," he said, teasing her. "But...you're escaping."

"Escaping...you might rightly say *so*, doctor. And I think you could call my case serious."

—

"Really? I'm sorry…"

"I was about to become engaged. But his family pressured him to call it off."

"Why did they do that?"

Vanessa looked at Dr. Roderigo so that he knew that she was not going to go into that now.

"Well," he shifted. "Perhaps it isn't too late to rescue the situation…in Brazil the youth are permitted to change their minds."

"No, I'm afraid it's quite ruined," said Vanessa. "Not a chance."

Vanessa flushed. She could not cry, not in front of this man she was supposed to be interviewing for a job. Not here. Not now. She saw him watching her closely, waiting to see what she would do.

Reversing field, she said nonchalantly, "I'm sure this isn't the time to go into my personal affairs in depth, Dr. Roderigo. As much as we are both interested in such things. To tell the truth, I'm about to head out for Buzios to join some nice people at a colleague's beach place. Don't you have weekend plans?"

"Uh, yes -- Ms. Saxe, I'm moving to a different apartment. You see, I too have a story, and mine is very sad: back in October my wife was struck by a car and killed. I have been getting ready to move to another flat, and now's the time."

Vanessa snapped out of her self-regard. She dropped all thoughts of Alvaro Fontes.

"I'm so sorry, Dr. Roderigo. You have no children, I'm reading here…"

"Not yet. That seems like a great blessing right now…"

"Yes—of course I can see why you might feel that way. But doctor, considering, wouldn't it be better if you came back Monday morning at 11? --- after you've comfortably set up your new household? I'll know I'll be in better spirits after a weekend away at the beach. Monday we can get down to work."

"Yes. I suppose that would be best…as a professional, I saw no reason to cancel our appointment today. Life must go on."

Vanessa nodded in accord. "Thank you for your concern, Dr. Roderigo. We'll see each other Monday morning, then? I hope your move-in won't be too difficult."

As the doctor left her office, Vanessa turned on her heel to review the magnificent bay. The sun had moved past Sugar Loaf, and soon would set famously over the Morro da Gavea, beyond Leblon Beach. Brazil, the Brazilians, she muttered half-aloud—will wonders never cease?

Vanessa picked up her weekend bags and went purposefully for the elevator, without switching off her office lights. Friends, drinks and the spectacular beach at Buzios awaited. She was not in the mood to cry any more.

2.

Most of the women who worked the waterfront would hurry their men up and down the stairs of the Hotel Florida, and be done with them. But Mariana was a little different; she'd been around the game forever and had

—

better manners. She looked nothing like her wicked fifty years.

"Come on now, black beauty," she heard a voice say.

"OK, baby, just a minute."

Almost New Year's and works to do. Mariana dropped her white towel and came out of the bathroom.

She thought of Dona Silvia de Moraes. How she had served Dona Silvia as a housemaid for almost a year. That ended about three months back with the poor lady's accidental death. Mariana was back on the streets.

"Baby," she spoke up abruptly, "can you believe that that crazy broad's husband was a doctor?" Grabbing the man's lighter, she quickly arranged a cigarette.

The man saw Mariana's enormously promising lips wrapped fiercely around the cancer stick; he saw her treading anger in smoke turned a fiendish purple by the neon hotel sign outside. The sharp angles of her angry African mask seemed to suck in the hazed purple tone.

The man asked, "Honey, you sound so angry. What kind of wild story *is* this you're thinking about this promising New Year's Eve?"

On the ground floor of the hotel the enormous speakers of the Bar Erotika wobbled and trembled with disco bass. The building shuddered. The Seventies were moving along.

"About Dona Silvia----poor thing."

"Who?"

"A first class lady I worked for…Dr. Roderigo's wife."

"And what happened with them?"

"She died, honey. Run down by a drunk on Avenida Barata Ribeiro."

"Poor thing…may she rest in peace."

"Exactly, there you've got it right, absolutely right. You're nice, honey—what was your name?"

"I'm Geraldo."

"Geraldo, listen here: we're going to enjoy a really hot and beautiful New Year's Eve together," Mariana said, watching her curling cigarette smoke. "We've got hours."

Geraldo's hands sought for her thigh, down the sheets where there was a little reflected neon.

The problem was that Dona Silvia couldn't give Dr. Roderigo a child, Mariana explained to Geraldo. While fertility treatments were virtually unheard of in Brazil, Dona Silvia frustrated her physician husband more so by refusing to submit to any diagnostic test. Meanwhile, she wanted a child, and she wanted sex.

"Listen close, Geraldo: That silver spoon fed Dona Silvia was a stubborn mule."

Geraldo could see it would be some kind of different New Year's Eve, for sure. Yeah, fine…a foolish story often goes well with a nice piece of ass. This wired-up broad has a great big swinging pair of black boobs. That wild look in her eye made promises. Her lips looked like a couple of soft pillows where you could rest that restless friend who lived in your pants.

Mariana could wait. She had manners. She rummaged in her little bag for another smoke.

Men, she thought. Even smart aleck Dr. Roderigo with his professor specs. Beside all the crap from Dona Silvia, he couldn't keep himself out of woman trouble. And finally, what terrible thing did he do?

Geraldo sat upright. "Are you a believer?" he asked Mariana.

"Believer---me? Pardon me but—not in that one dumb ass God. A daughter of Iemanja, I might be. I've been known to light a few candles and dance with my saint. And you?"

He was a Catholic. It worried him considerably that she might have lit some candles that very night. Bloody Exu, that horrid little imp, would be opening pathways providing strong works in her favor during the oncoming New Year. That stuff frightened Geraldo, but hookers were hookers, and not meant to last. He had a wife he loved up in Fortaleza. He had Mariana and this hotel bed for his New Year's treat. But now he was a little scared.

Geraldo remembered hearing about a man who wanted his wife killed. A week later, the guy turned up in the morning during Copacabana garbage collection, falling out of a can with his throat slashed from ear to ear, so that when they lifted him up, his head fell off. They said one had made the correct approach to the demons to make the other man pay. What for, he didn't recall.

"Come a little closer, won't you, luscious," Geraldo said, looking to put the image of the man's severed head behind him.

Mariana pivoted suddenly to regard the man stretched out at arms' length. And he saw her: in purple light and amateur shadow, the full array: big breasts, dark flashing arms, her face angled the same as some fearsome Congo mask. She slid down on the mattress to lie next to him on her stomach, smelling faintly of pitch, like a big tanker docking in midnight fog.

She looked into his face. 'I wonder,' thought Mariana, 'how much this guy Geraldo here thinks the gods and saints involve themselves with mankind? He goes to confession, maybe, the morning after he spends a very busy night with me. And considering men--such as they were--it wasn't surprising that Olorun, Big Daddy, long ago retired beyond the pale to Heaven on High, where gods aren't bothered by what they start. Mighty Orangun ran after his mother Iemanja, milady. She fell flat and the rivers that spilt from her deflated tits bore Xango, Oxala, Ogun and the rest---our Gods! What a mess: these days most folks you meet can't even get the names straight. But I can prove something to this Geraldo—you'd better believe that.

She thought, 'Hell, I'll never quit being angry when I think about how they chained us blackies in the holds of

ships and brought us here—that's right, here, to Brazil-- to cut their damn mahogany and bloody cane. English, Dutch, French, it didn't matter—the masters of our country, the Portuguese. Whip hand. Well, I'm not done with them yet!

'No problem for those Portuguese Prince Henry Navigators, fucking slave girls.

—

'So how did we fight back? We blacks had to hide our glorious religion behind plaster saints! Call Ogun Saint George? You kidding me? What did Africans know about dragons! Calling that little bogeyman of the crossroad Exu 'the devil,' that was really too much of a joke!

'It's no wonder they don't make the right approach. They think of macumba magic as so much crap. Candles lit on the corner on Monday nights. When they see grain dusted in the gutter to please a saint those dimwits say, 'Wouldn't it be better if those people didn't waste food, the hungry fools!'

'Right out in the middle of the cobble-stoned street: chickens with necks snapped! Who knows? Take it seriously!

'Believe me, the gods want things done right.

'Some say it's all quacks, like the ones Dona Silvia got herself involved with. Sure, they'll take your money to explain it. For a fee. For a fee they'll tell you that you can receive a saint and dance like a dervish that very evening. With no initiation. With no training. Oh you--handsome young man, and you--little dried up Grand Dad: they'll sell you a potion and a poem to make her dream of you. She'll buy that soap, *The Dream of Nymphs,* take a beauty bath, and sit and wait on the edge of the bed. Dona Silvia did.

'Some fools say you can receive Oxala—no one ever has! Liars! Cheats! Quacks! They try to spoil our magic for a fee.

'That's right Mr. gitty-up Geraldo, there's magic all right, for good or for whatever. Maybe you're worried about the stories in the *Jornal do Brasil,* where somebody goes down an alleyway to light a candle and never comes back.

Mugged, raped, robbed. So much for that. That's not the fault of your so-called black magic—well, not always.

'And me, here I am in the name of Love. On New Year's Eve, Mr. Geraldo comes to me. Just an ancient whore, that's all I am, an old black, black magic witch. Right?'

"You know, maybe you could say it *was* suicide, with Dona Silvia," Mariana said aloud now, resolutely.

"Could be," said Geraldo. "But listen, Mariana— love is here," he moved her hand to his stiff joint, "and woman, where are you?"

"Just listen to this: Dona Silvia—she was such a lousy driver, she once got into an accident right in front of Dr. Roderigo's office building, where his medical practice was located. She went upstairs and sat down in the waiting room...."

"Hey, you big bountiful thing---come on now, please, right now, woman come here and let's play. Stop with this soap opera of who she was and he was and what they did. I don't even know who you're talking about!"

Mariana put a ruling hand on Geraldo's shoulder. "Of course, that was just like her," she said to him directly.

"Her name was Dona Silvia de Moraes. For the love of God mister, who else?"

3.

—

Now, you can see that I try to dress well and look good and sharp on the street. I have my spot, ya know, the stand where I solder together the little metal Exus I sell. My shoes are always shined. You know all about Exu and macumba, I'm sure, right detective? Well, the foreigners call my little statues devils. Sure, he has a pitchfork and pointy ears but although you know he can make shit happen, he is not exactly your Christian fiend.

You know all about macumba, right detective, but I waste a shitload of time explaining some facts to the visitors.

"No, not devil, not devil," I tell them. That's it for me when it comes to English. I try to explain how Exu's the strange cat that has to be dealt with before you can get to work with the other macumba saints. If you don't spill the blood of a chicken or a goat Exu does dirty tricks. (I leave out the part where he sometimes does nasty business anyway-- you know what I mean, detective.)

The whiteys say, "Saints wouldn't work with that voodoo devil!"

"No, not devil, not devil!"

After all that wordplay many foreigners buy my Exu, saying, "OK, I'll take that cute little devil—how much?"

If it is a devil, I feel sorry for them. It goes back to London or Miami to do its thing…You want to know what my little Exu looks like?

Let's see…He's very typical: not six inches high. Sometimes I have made them taller, special order. It's all made out of ¼" thick iron wire rusted a dark brown. The body is one piece with the tail angled back. At home I hammer the bottom of the tailpiece flat, so Exu can stand upright. That is, once his legs, another single piece of wire bent like an upside-down V, are attached to the trunk. Can you visualize that, comrade? With legs on there is a solid base, because the bottom of the legs are beaten into flat feet that face front.

The arms and hands are also a single piece. It gets attached at a point below the neck. Look here: the arms end in round holes so Exu can hold his pike with one hand, and with the other, his trident. Now he looks noble, except he doesn't have a head.

The head is tough because you have to scrape gashes in the metal to show eyes and mouth. You solder on a bump for a nose. The long ears are also soldered on. That's work I sometimes do on the street; it's good for sales to be putting the pieces together where folks can see.

Then I set the little man up and say, "There, look how handsome he is, how dignified—such a dark gentleman. How elegant, my Exu. Powerful too."

They say, "It won't fall apart?"

"Oh, no…"

"It won't hurt my family if I take it to my house?" They laugh when they say that.

"No, ma'am."

—

"OK, I'll take one of those little devils, then…"

"No, not devil, not devil!"

Yes, many have their minds made up about Exu. He likes to drink a lot of cachaca and smoke the finest, fattest cigars. He lies, uses foul language and gross gestures when he's offended, and he chases every female ass. All those dirty tricks! But they shouldn't be fooled by Exu's terrible reputation. The everyday world doesn't matter to him; all he does is open the door so more work can be done. The doorman at the Saints' and Sorcerers' Club, funny huh?

Don't forget that all this time, Exu is a king, a god. No matter what he does, his black shoes are kept perfectly polished. He prefers to act the gent. A gentleman, like the guys you meet in the Carnival with red-trimmed black satin tuxedos and top hats.

So what was I saying?

OK, under the counter of my stand I have sometimes kept other things. I'll buy stuff from guys who took it, when they have to unload it on the run. I resell it for them. It's a good deal. I'll admit it—anyway, that's all a matter of record with the local police.

That is my system and it keeps me going. Believe me, I'm not mixed up in a lot of other jazz.

What are you talking about---that Vanessa? You guys know the way it was when I ran into her: she wanted me to explain something I know plenty about, right?

4.

Vanessa Saxe was no stranger to the sea; her late father had been a consular official in Belize, where he took the family to live for two years beginning when Vanessa was five and her sister Tess was just an infant. The sea for certain: In Rio you could sail and swim and of course spend entire days with your bum parked on Ipanema beach while you gabbed with friends. In a bikini, lanky Vanessa Saxe looked as good as almost any girl from Ipanema, and she likewise regarded the seaside with romantic expectation.

There had been so many good times on Alvaro's sailboat, but that was over; she didn't want to think about it.

Now she was driving with Hilton, her helpful chum from Bright and Peters who had a fat salary, a fast car, and a serious drinking problem. They were heading out three hours from Rio to the beach at Buzios. Hilton was well launched on another weekend bender, and Vanessa, who was no chicken, rode with a stiff arm against the dash.

"Watch it, mate!"

"I prefer to watch you, Vanessa!"

Well, it was just a three-hour ride, the way Hilton drove. The salt flats were beastly hot. The hot air wavered in the distance. The windmills barely turned.

When there was no conversation, Vanessa couldn't help thinking about Dr. Roderigo de Moraes. Try as she might she just couldn't seem to block him out. Why would the fellow want to become a medical consultant to the firm so soon after his wife dies? Perhaps he wanted a challenge, change, to take his mind off of his loss. She felt very curious about his wife's death, and she didn't quite understand why, seeing how it was nothing but a mindless

—

auto accident. This mystery took her mind off of Alvaro Fontes, for goodness sake!

Hilton turned the car hard, onto a brief, tight bridge that led from the town of Cabo Frio onto the Buzios peninsula. Everything was awash in brilliant bending sunlight.

Frequent bumps made them joggle like Punch and Judy.

"Why don't they give some bugger the job he needs fixing this bridge?" Hilton growled.

"Amen to that, mate. You know how Brazil is."

Toasting to that, Hilton spilled whiskey onto his gearshift. Both of them laughed.

Soon, there were Brahma cattle grazing vast grassy fields. For Vanessa, this animal scenery signaled the real beginning of the weekend: Buzios was close by. Thank goodness! Working with personnel in Brazil could be a pain in the butt. What lunatic excuses she had to listen to, day-in, day-out! A bloody mystery made out of everything. She, who tried her best to never stop making sense, could use a rest.

Their clique had rented a place for November thru February, the hottest Brazilian months. The pink beach house sat just ten meters from the water's edge. It wasn't large: Vanessa thought of it as a kind of dollhouse, but the cottage did have an oversize front window that perfectly framed their tiny cove beach. Towards the right hand side of the picture, a couple of little desert-beige hills lifted themselves gently. These hills were studded with pale cactus. Looking that way, you saw that the rocks came right down to the water's edge. You could not pass that way, through the pounding surf.

Beyond those sandy hills a dark mountain rose higher still; you could get a good glimpse of a house up there that belonged to Brigitte Bardot. One never saw her, however. Never mind, the group's own beach was picture perfect.

Vanessa finished putting her things into a tiny bedroom and came back to the living area to slouch in a comfortable wicker chair. On the big front window, the setting sun painted a soft crimson watercolor, a lucent blush.

Finally, her mind quit working overtime. "The reward of the hardworking person," she said to Hilton, who was occupied fixing himself another cocktail.

"Wonder where the others are?" Hilton asked.

"Probably gone for a swim 'round the other side," Vanessa said.

She dreaded being alone in the house too long with Hilton, who now that he knew it was over between her and Alvaro Fontes, would begin to 'console' her when he was

adequately soused. Not a bad fellow, mind you—except with the steady drinking he didn't appeal. But he was functional: Vanessa was well acquainted with the details of Hilton's innovative work performance, and she knew his salary figure to the pound. He had been with High and Peters in Rio for seven years. Yes, he did need someone, Vanessa knew—if one day a woman appeared who she thought could handle the task that was Hilton, she might attempt to match them.

—

"Paws off, mate," she said. No Hilton, no thanks.

"Les go 'round see if we can find 'em, Ness..."

"It's a little late, Hilton. It might be dark if it takes an hour to track them down."

"Grab ourselves a coupla torches, Bright and Peters!"

It wasn't hard to locate flashlights and for Hilton to find a big plastic beach cup for his rum and coke.

"All right, then Hilton, out we go. Maybe we'll meet the others on their way back."

After twenty minutes walking along the shell-strewn flat, where the surf played out against the last light, they caught a glimpse of their good friend Richard alongside a big blonde man.

Richard Smithson, the most prosperous man in their group and a Senior Vice President at B and P, Rio had taken charge of the Buzios rental. He was generous and very gay.

"D'we know that blonde fellow?" asked Hilton, spilling Cuba Libre on the sand.

"Not yet, we don't. Careful there, mate."

At five meters you saw flippers, a mask and snorkel dangling from the stranger's hand. Even after a week at the beach, their friend Richard looked snow-white next to him. The big Scandinavian had evidently been spending many long days in Brazil. In the sun. Swim fins were a good sign.

"Richard didn't mention having someone else out, did 'e, Ness?"

"They must've found one another down here."

Very few of the men Richard picked up turned out to be gay. Their friend would go after anyone who looked tasty, and was generally as pleased as punch to pass his prospects along.

The pairs met.

"Hello there—how was the trip?" Richard asked.

"Fine," Vanessa answered, frowning.

"A lovely week I've had here," said Richard. "But let me introduce you newcomers to Gunnar."

Vanessa had never seen a Swede turned such a deep bronze. Gunnar was past sunburned with a brighter pinkish hot spot only here and there.

"Glad to meet you---" she said, giving Gunnar the long look, "It's a pity the rest of us are just weekenders here."

"Neither pity, nor pleasure," Richard replied. "Hilton, how are you? How was the drive?"

"Can't really recall. Can you--?" He turned to Vanessa.

The English laughed, and Gunnar laughed.

"Been here long?" Vanessa asked him.

"Yuh, a whole mont' by myself on a liddle beach over dot hill. I sleep in a dent."

"A tent then, how wonderful," said Vanessa zestfully. "You're traveling solo, are you?"

—

"Yuh, I'm away from Sweden two years now…"

"Join us for dinner this time, please, now that these others have arrived," said Richard.

"I must change clothes."

"Oh, no," said Richard. He stepped forward, taking Hilton's arm and threatening to sashay all the way back to the beach house. "You're just fine as you are."

Vanessa and Gunnar trailed behind. Before reaching the cottage, they caught sight of the few lights of the village of Buzios, several hundred meters inland. The rented cottage was not much further along. A sandhill behind it blocked the view of the village. At the moment, the mosquitoes did not seem to be hungry. Settling darkness was feeling wonderfully cool and sea-sprayed after a near-one-hundred-degree late December Rio day.

"I have been able to spear a lot of fish while I snorkel," Gunnar told Vanessa.

"And they're cooking up well, I suppose?" Vanessa said she had noticed some piles of burned up firewood.

Gunnar chuckled and his taut stomach muscles gained profile. "Yuh, that's mine; I eat a lot of fish!"

Both of them laughed.

"I even find some secret things," Gunnar said, making a foolish attempt at a madman's expression.

"What's that about mate?" Vanessa raised an eyebrow.

"Did you ever go over dese hills?" Gunnar pointed beyond the cottage.

"Once or twice. It's difficult to go that way."

"Vell yah—I went over, and about a kilometer past. I climb over some rough rocks and find a beautiful spot of beach, only four meters wide, with a cave. I saw some broken candles, seashells and little junks inside, but it's nice and smooth rock and calm to sit, since the water flows in the cave mouth gently, and comes up to your knees. But then I hear an odd noise and so I leave. It sounded like—I would call it—laughing."

"Hmn… glad that was funny! You must show me later! You say the cave had ritual stuff inside? That's beginning to interest to me now, Gunnar, because after four years, I'm beginning to think one can't live in Brazil and without knowing about their sort of 'black magic'."

"Yah, maybe it is so," Gunnar said, a bit uncomfortably, "But I don't think I will want to go tonight, when it will be so dark. The rocks are a liddle too slippery. Tomorrow, maybe, we go…"

"Come on, mate...you don't look like the type to be scared by a few candles."

"Vell, no…Listen, Vanessa, tomorrow on that beach, we can sunbathe nude. Nobody will see."

"That certainly is fine with me, mate. You have a deal."

Vanessa was ready to have a good time with a hunk. There had been no one since Alvaro. She was not enjoying being 'available' again with all the unwelcome business that entailed. Meanwhile, this Gunnar was rugged, a swimmer,

—

and he seemed cool. Like the Brazilians would say on Friday night, 'Then…it's Saturday morning for us?'

Hilton and Richard had reached the cottage. They were on the porch. Their loud cackles spoiled Vanessa's fantasy.

"OK, what's the laugh--you bloody Neanderthals," she cried.

There was no answer to that. "Come on up," Hilton called.

"Listen, they're very nice people," Vanessa said nervously to Gunnar. "But Hilton has a bit of a problem with alcohol."

"Yah, I notice from his breath. Too bad for him. It never comes out good."

"Yes, that's so; drink is fine, but not the way he does it…"

"Yah, nothing wrong with a couple of Brahma beers from Brazil. I like beer, and I like that Brahma."

"Me too. So let's grab a chilly one before dinner."

Sitting on the porch of the cottage with their beers, Vanessa paused to tell Gunnar how she'd once shown up early for a dinner party at Hilton's, only to find the host sprawled on the floor cushions at his flat, out cold, still dressed in his lovely pale grey, pin-striped, three-piece office day suit. A colorful caipirinha cocktail had spilled across the polished hardwood floor. Hilton's maid was in the kitchen, going about her business.

"Come, let me help you up, you basket-case," Vanessa had said. Forty-five minutes later, the maid served dinner to twelve people. Hilton managed to sit up straight.

She thought, 'With Hilton as with others, there is a limit to what one can do.'

As if to confirm that, when she finished the story Gunnar only shrugged.

Then all of the guests were in the living room of the cottage, toasting one another's health. Richard's maid, who always came down with him to Buzios, passed through the room carrying a steam iron.

"Oh, Sonia! Don't tell me—We're having iron for dinner," Richard joked.

Everyone laughed. B and P people always laughed heartily at Richard Smithson's jokes. Nice, it seemed to Vanessa--when everyone laughed, Gunnar laughed too.

The drinking went on with dinner, a shrimp-laden Bahian seafood stew. Vanessa enjoyed the fact that Gunnar was such a terrific sport. He worked so very hard to be good company amidst the Bright and Peters clique. A couple of years on the road must have made him light on his feet with folks, if you could say such of someone the size of this serene Ajax.

Shortly after the meal was over, Hilton passed out in a chair.

Vanessa immediately said, "Richard, can you and Gunnar kindly move him to a bedroom? The sight of him makes me want to weep."

—

"Yes, I understand. A good idea, love. Gunnar?"

The evening wound down. Vanessa offered to walk with Gunnar along the beach in the direction of his tent. The alternative stars spangled the Southern sky, and she hoped for something exciting to occur.

At a certain point, she felt she must take matters in hand.

"Let's go, mate," she said. Pulling off her bikini, she crashed into the waves. In a moment, Gunnar was there. Both were strong swimmers, and their starlit bodies glistened in the surf, and then, in the sand. A loving tussle began between the blonde and the redhead and they were working up a tropical sweat and a coating of sand, when Gunnar backed off.

"I cand," he said.

"You're saying what?"

"I cand make love wit you, Vanessa."

"Oh - Oh—got a girlfriend, is it?' Her lips savagely curled, like Mick Jagger's.

"No, no. I hardly know how to tell you."

"Tell me what, Gunnar?"

"Listen to me, please Vanessa. A few days ago, I was snorkeling out here, when something attacked me. It vas big. It came up under me. I thought, oh, no, it's a shark; I will be a dead man. But under the water it looked strange, not like a shark, but something green and red. I thought I heard it laugh! Then it came up and hit me. It give me a nice wallop right down in the swim pants. I swear I heard it laugh again. Still hurts."

"You're joking, mate," Vanessa said, but Gunnar showed her. His entire crotch area was clearly and seriously bruised. His erection was gone.

"No, that doesn't look funny to me," said Vanessa. "But you haven't gone for help?"

"I don't vant to go back to the city right now. Yesterday I told some fishermen I heard this creature laugh, then it attack me," Gunnar explained.

"And?"

"The guys around here are really crazy; they are always smoking the stuff, you know. They said it must have been 'homen marinho,' some monster that comes up from the sea to attack the privates of men."

"The privates of men…" she repeated.

And then she thought, No, not again. Vanessa was exploding...Not another Brazilian fairy tale! One a day is quite sufficient.'

"Gunnar, I'm going back to the cottage now," she said.

He held out his golden arms. "Please Vanessa, I'm so sorry about it—dat stupid stuff, I didn't even want to tell," he said.

Covered with sweat and sand Vanessa was gone before he could become more sentimental. She quickly headed along the dark beach for the cottage, two scant slices of bikini dangling from her right hand.

—

The hot trip with the big Swede was off. 'The tryst of the cozy slippery enchanted cave is definitely not on for tomorrow,' she notified herself.

5.

A girl leaned against the door of the hotel room Geraldo had paid for, and said, as loudly and quietly as possible: "Stay in the room, Mariana! Don't come out of there, no. The police are everywhere tonight…"

In the room, Mariana sat up in bed, listening.

"Looking for who?" she asked, but the girls didn't know.

Downstairs, grey uniformed officers moved brusquely through the Bar Erotika, shoving customers aside, searching for someone. Sub-machine guns were held at angles, ready for disturbance.

On the walls Day-Glo paintings of elegant green mermaids and overdeveloped, masked Carnival dancers were lit by purplish black light.

Men, seated at tables of four or five, or milling around, watched the stage at the back of the big room. There girls with skin hues all colors of the rainbow shook their stuff to disco tunes. Sometimes, when the music switched to a samba, the girls sang along. It would be Carnival in a couple of months, and people were learning the year's song lyrics. Some of the girls dancing on the stage would give each other passionate kisses and giggle. Thursday nights a few girls stripped off their clothes and made love.

Otherwise a girl would be busy wandering the floor to visit tables, introducing herself to the men.

"Hi, Mister, I'm Aracy. How are you tonight? Would you like to buy me a drink? We can sit here and talk, nice and relaxed." At that, Aracy's lips and tongue tip would come up close to the man's earlobe, as she began to make good on her calming bossa nova promise and develop her fee.

Mariana and Geraldo had already made love once. He wanted to do it another time, so he could take her from behind.

Mariana thought, 'If the girls out there were right, it is best not to hurry. Right Mariana. Fine. Stay here with Geraldo, this good fellow, safe and sound.'

"Hey Geraldo--how about a cigarette for us to share--?' she said.

Geraldo flopped over.

"Sure."

Smoking, Mariana told him how the business got under way in Dona Silvia's kitchen. She and her workmate Ruth were cutting onions and carrots for a soup.

Thin-lipped Dona Silvia came to the doorway and said, "Not ready yet? You'd better hurry, you two hare brains—cut the fofoca. Dr. Roderigo will be home any minute."

"Yes, ma'am."

Silvia headed back to the living room.

—

"I feel so sorry for Dona Silvia," said Ruth under her breath. "A woman whose husband is a doctor should be the best one to raise a child."

"She needs to have one first," said Mariana.

"I bet Dona Elva could help her…"

"Who's that—Dona who?" Mariana asked.

"A macumbeira up there in Recife where I'm from, Dona Elva. She told me to get out and come to Rio after what happened with my man, remember?"

Mariana had heard the story.

"And what would your Dona Elva have for our poor Silvia de Moraes?"

Ruth blushed a red like no color in Brazil.

"Out with it, don't be silly."

Ruth timidly said, "You know about 'witches' coffee' right?"

Mariana looked down her nose. "Maybe I do, girlfriend, but do me a favor: go ahead, you tell me."

Ruth lowered her voice. "Dona Elva said to take the nightgown you wore while you were bleeding and strain your man's morning coffee through it. After that, a child would come. I mean, after the man drinks…"

Mariana cut her off, laughing aloud. "And she said it worked every time?"

Dona Silvia was standing in the kitchen doorway, listening in. "What beastly stuff!" she said. "You two had better stop that right now...I mean, stop with that type of talk, and get our dinner cooked. You like your jobs here, right?"

"Yes, ma'am. We're finishing."

"That's absolutely horrible, girls," Silvia added. "Don't tell me a man wouldn't taste it!"

"Not really," said Mariana, not looking up from stirring soup.

"Ah, I see, Mariana--it had to be you."

"Had to be me, Dona Silvia?"

The elevator could be heard arriving at their floor. Silvia darted for the foyer.

"Sorry," said Ruth.

"Forget it. Go set the table, butt-face, soup's ready."

Here and now, Geraldo was with Mariana, and he said, "I know the type—that's a couple who were probably married in the pretty little Nossa Senhora da Gloria church, on that hillside over the beach. They had everything else you could want, right? How beautiful!"

"Exactly—you know their kind of gente fina, huh Geraldo?"

"Yeah-I drove a taxi for a while."

There was a fight in the de Moraes apartment every night. Roderigo couldn't get Silvia to go for a fertility exam.

—

"Don't worry dear, it will work out all right," Silvia would say.

"No, no it won't. It's been two years, Silvinha, dear." Every night to repair things, she wanted to make love.

"Roderigo, I know there's nothing wrong with me."

Dr. Roderigo had gone to a colleague for a test a month into their marriage and was told he had no problem. He was the proud adopted son of a Minas landowner, and he was just 37. Silvia would never accept a divorce.

"Mariana---Dona Silvia says you and Ruth are irritating her with your crazy talk," Dr. Roderigo said one night when he was eating dinner solo.

"I'm sorry sir; we don't mean any harm. You must excuse us; maybe we're just a little ignorant. Are you ready for dessert?"

"Yes, ignorant. Meanwhile, cut that mumbo-jumbo out if you want to stay in this household, get it? You're hearing me clearly, no confusion, am I right? Now, uh--Do we have any doce de leite for dessert?"

"So Dona Silvia finally did start up..." Geraldo guessed.

That's right, Silvia was aware that lighting candles on corners at dusk was something plenty of gente fina did, it wasn't only housemaids.

"You know, after all that time, poor Silvia was desperate. She started asking us questions every day."

Geraldo sat up. He looked out of the dirty window, seeing how the clashing neon lights of the Praca Maua distorted the lines of the speeding city buses.

"Plenty of cops out there tonight," he said.

"Is that right? Must be like any other New Year's Eve."

"No, not exactly Mariana, my beautiful mulatta: this year it's right here, you and me—so how about some more of your tasty chocolate--?"

Geraldo quit the window and found a generous welcome in Mariana's ebony embrace.

Anything but the cops.

6.

Brazilian Special Security Forces Report, Jan. 3, continuing transcript of the questioning of Mel Androu, street vendor

So there we were, after the ceremony, a bunch of us stuck in that delegacia with the damn local pigs scaring the

shit out of everybody: the old ladies with their white petticoats and anybody who didn't take off over the hill when the bastards snapped on their searchlights. What did I get for my kindness, for the trouble I took? Down here at the stationhouse with the rest!

Ain't that so, friend? I'm sorry, because I don't mean to insult you personally, you're not like those other cheap cops.

—

I remember how I saw Red standing in the clearing with some glasses-wearing gente fina. I could have got away, 'cause I had a feeling the man was about to arrive. But one look and I had to help. Had to help her. You saw that red hair, so you know what I mean, OK?

Right away I told your officers I had never been around one of those macumba magic scenes. That was a fat lie. It's just that they had picked me up before, for theft and such, so I didn't want to complicate matters. Anyway, they put a number of us into their police vans, and we came here.

'How dare you!' was all you heard from the gente fina, besides how he was a doctor of something or nothing, and how could they hold him in that cruddy stationhouse, waiting around like the rest of the trash. You don't think he felt the cops should offer the privilege of rapid processing to me, Mel, do you? I know for certain that I don't have any critical cases to rush out and treat.

Red had a few things to say to the cops, like, 'Can you please tell us what we're being held here for?' She got upset and starting talking English. Didn't she know those cops don't understand a word that makes sense?

OK, hey I'm sorry, put your baton down please-- take it easy. I don't mean to offend.

Of course, detective, your colleagues the respectable delegates of the local force wanted to see everybody's papers. They started copying, but they're not going fast. They're paid by the month not by the word, am I right? If a guy doesn't do anything for a month he's glad. He's a month closer to retirement, and he's still alive. Am I right? Unless he gets tired of riding around in a black van in the midday sun scaring the shit out of everyone, or sitting around the station tv, looking at futebol and yapping about

Rivelino or Zico just like the jerks on the street who aren't carrying submachine guns. Then he might do some police work, just for kicks.

Ya know, I been there before. I got the bruises to show. I'm sorry, I can't stop feeling a little angry, because I did nothing wrong. I'll try to continue.

Gentleman that I am, I felt I had to try to explain to Red what we were dealing with.

"Don't make so much fuss, Miss," I said. "You'll just get these 'gentlemen' of the police angry."

She looked at me sideways and grinned. She liked that, I saw. She could understand Portuguese!

"I can't believe it's a crime just watching one macumba meeting," she told me. "People are playing music and dancing, after all."

I tried to explain that neither the cops nor the gods cared who was watching a macumba ceremony and who was participating. I asked her name.

"Vanessa," she said. "And you?"

"Mel Androu is what they call me."

"So, Mel, let me see if I have this right—you're saying that just being present means being involved, did I get it?"

I wanted to oblige her, you know the score, but I couldn't figure out which way she wanted it to break. "It's possible," I said, "If you're open."

"Open?"

—

At that point her doctor friend, the gente fina, stepped up.

"Nonsense," he said in a loud voice, "we were there looking for someone who worked for my family, nothing more."

"It's all the same to me," I told him. "But if you and Red pipe down maybe the respectable delegates here will give us all a better shake."

"You've got some nerve talking to me like that!" He claimed he was one Dr. Roderigo de Moraes.

"Friend," I told him, "you're making about as much of an impression with these cops as you are with me. Put a sock in that medical mouth of yours, please!"

"You lousy piece of trash," he started to say, but Vanessa spoke to him in English and he clammed up. They went on that way, talking 'kwa-kwa-kwa' in English, and answering 'qua-qua-qua' back. Meanwhile your street cops slowly copied our papers, hoping to reach retirement before they were done.

Detective, I feel for those local guys because I was getting sick of the smell of piss in their stationhouse.

We'd soon be out, I figured, as they'd just hold a few of the Daughters of the Saints who were dressed in their numerous layers of white petticoats and like, billowing hoop skirts. Just a night in the clink for some poor old bat who is unlucky enough to be thrashing around joyfully in the arms of her Pai Xango when cops come around. What does she care for the uniforms of the state, the forces of Order and Progress? On the other hand, the cops have some use for those old dames. Their lists can always handle a few more suspects; maybe that's how they get paid--you know better I'm sure, sir, by the suspect?

"Not funny?"

Red and the loudmouth doctor were going on with their English lesson. Each one would blast away. "Kwa-kwa. No, kwa-kwo." Then Doc threw his hands up and Red walked over my way.

"He's saying I'm a fool for talking to you," she said.

"I can see what he thinks. So, that's your call," I told her.

"Right, so I want to ask you--What did you mean?"

"What?"

"When you said that it didn't matter to the gods who was watching and who was involved—what exactly did that mean?"

"Get your better-educated friend to explain."

"Please, you might know more than he does about this," she said, "I don't intend to argue with you as well."

Yeah, she was tough, I saw. "All right," I said. "The gods work with anyone who's open to their influence, get it?"

Then she shocked me cold. "Sometimes these days I think your Brazilian gods must have something in store for me. Is that too ridiculous?"

"With all respect...I don't know you, not a bit, Miss."

—

"But macumba—you know something about that."

I told her about my work with little Exu statuettes, and how I sold them every day to folks similar to her kind downtown near Av. Rio Branco. I said I had a number of macumba contacts around the city.

That prick Dr. Roderigo was looking my way as if he was ready to operate on me without even a blunt and filthy knife. He would open me up with his thumbs. The man could certainly kill as well as he could heal.

Vanessa noticed too. "Could we talk another time, Mel?" she asked, as casual as could be.

"Sure."

So: that Vanessa slipped me a card with her business address and asked me to call. That would be, what do you figure, detective—around Dec. 10--three weeks ago?

7.

Promptly at 11 am on Monday, Dr. Roderigo de Moraes reported to Vanessa's office.

"How was your weekend, Ms. Saxe?" he asked. "Feeling any better?"

Vanessa didn't answer quickly. She was depressed and disturbed by the events involving Gunnar. She wondered what possible animal attack would account for the painful bruise he showed her, without any cut? Had they played a joke on her? Could Richard Smithson and Hilton be capable of staging such a theatrical hoax, considering that they knew quite well that she was already suffering intensely over Alvaro Fontes? Why would they be that cruel?

Vanessa had stuck to the beach, sunbathing alone nearly full time Saturday and Sunday morning before returning from Buzios with Hilton. She did not wish to be drawn out about her scene with Gunnar by her B & P colleagues. If it were a nasty trick, she wasn't going to help them gloat.

"Actually, you look a little sunburned. Is it painful Ms. Saxe?" Dr. Roderigo said, returning Vanessa to the here and now.

"Right—I don't feel one hundred per cent. People with pale skin like mine can burn even if they're well-tanned—but of course, you know that."

"Red-heads burn easily, it's true. You're sure that hasn't made you feel ill?"

"No, yes: I don't feel so great; I did say that. Took aspirin for a headache. Hold on a minute; I've almost forgotten that I had a question for you: something that came up over weekend. I'm almost embarrassed to say, but here you go: have you ever heard some nonsense about 'homen marinho'?"

Dr. Roderigo felt like a small fire had ignited. He had no idea where it was but did his best to control the flame. Here was a new 'patient,' a very attractive Englishwoman, across the desk from him.

"Yes, I know what you're talking about," he said. "It's another of the things some of us Brazilians believe in that in reality doesn't exist. Why do you ask?"

—

"I'm half-embarrassed really...You're sure that there are absolutely no documented cases?"

'What does she expect to hear?' Dr. Roderigo wondered.

He said, "There have been reports—of course, Ms. Saxe. Meanwhile, in Brazil there are hundreds of stories of flying saucers weekly, stories about broken teacups telling peoples' fortunes, and instant miracle cures performed by cross-eyed quacks. Brazilians are believers...May I ask again why you take an interest?"

Vanessa admitted that after four years in Rio, she had become aware that talk of the magical dimension seemed unavoidable. In her work, she needed to be a careful student of people, she said.

"Yes, naturally."

Then she reported on the evening with Gunnar in Buzios.

"So you actually saw a severe bruise?" asked the doctor.

"Quite severe. But no cuts."

"Ms. Saxe, I think this Swedish fellow was very lucky. It sounds to me like he collided with a shark which was concentrating on something else in the water."

"Could be. Some fishermen told him the homen marinho stories."

"A bunch of strung-out potheads who never leave the beach having a joke at the foreigner's expense; isn't that probable?"

"I suppose so," said Vanessa. With that she slid from her chair onto the office floor.

After what she understood to be a few moments she found Dr. Roderigo leaning over her. It seemed he had been giving her smelling salts. An office porter and a secretary assisted. In the midst of regaining consciousness, she dreamily asked, 'Is there a nice man?'

Sitting up, Vanessa asked, "What happened, Dr. Roderigo?"

"You fainted, Ms. Saxe. Very likely that sunburn after all."

Vanessa hastened to get back into her seat. She drank several glasses of water and swallowed three more aspirin, according to the doctor's orders.

The others left the office. Vanessa sat there in silence with Dr. Roderigo. She was angry with herself.

After a couple of moments watching her, he asked, "Feeling any better?"

Vanessa nodded.

"Have you eaten a good meal since you returned from Buzios?"

"Now that you mention it, doctor, I didn't have much of a breakfast. And last night, we got in really late. I went straight to bed."

"Your firm must have a cafeteria, Ms. Saxe? Because I'm sure we can get you something and you will be feeling better very soon."

—

"I think you've got the right idea," said Vanessa, getting up from her desk as steadily as she could. After a few bites of lunch, she did find herself feeling much more solid.

Dr. Roderigo saw that this was so, and said to her, "As far as macumba is concerned, can I tell you what happened to my wife, Ms. Saxe?"

Vanessa smiled. "Yes, doctor. I think you owe me a few words there, after what you told me on Friday afternoon. And by the way, I have to ask: did your apartment move go well…"

"Of course." Dr. Roderigo said, and then launched into the story of Dona Silvia and her housemaids' superstitious advice.

"Ghastly," said Vanessa with gusto. She felt quite recovered. "So you actually drank that awful brew?"

"If only these ridiculous things worked! But that wasn't the end of it. Some idiotic fortune teller told Silvia that the cause of her sterility was that I had slept with Mariana, who might be 'doing works' against us."

"That peculiar old lady who worked in your kitchen? Isn't *that* some obnoxious balderdash!"

"Of course. But by then my wife couldn't handle the stress. As I told you when I came in on Friday, that back on October 5, my Silvia was crossing Avenida Barata Ribeiro near our flat when a car struck her. She died instantly. An eye-witness said Silvia had stopped right there, in the middle of a four-lane wide avenue—that it seemed like she was thinking about something else. A man shouted for her to watch out, but evidently she heard nothing."

"I'm so sorry, Dr. Roderigo. I suppose she was preoccupied. We are both victims of macumba magic, after a fashion, aren't we?"

Dr. Roderigo allowed himself to smile. "Thank you, Ms. Saxe. You might say so."

"I think you'll be feeling better now that you've moved from the place where you and Dona Silvia lived."

"You're right. I expect."

Noticing the wall clock, Vanessa abruptly said, "Dr. Roderigo—We've been here for hours. I need to get back upstairs. Thanks so much for your kindness. I'll call you by week's end, all good?"

"I look forward to your call. Good afternoon, Ms. Saxe. Try to relax a bit."

The following Wednesday afternoon Vanessa telephoned Dr. Roderigo's practice. She told him she wanted to talk to him further about the consulting position and suggested an after-work drink together at a hotel bar on

hectic Avenida Atlantica in Copacabana. She could proceed home to her flat in nearby Leme from there.

He was on time, and soon surprised her.

"I've decided to spend some time looking for Mariana," he said. "After unpacking things in my new flat, I felt uncomfortable. I felt I had to take some action to feel less uncomfortable about Silvia's death. There were a couple of bracelets in little case that I had given her for an anniversary gift. I thought they were being sent to her mother's place. It was painful, Vanessa".

—

He felt suspicious about the way Silvia had been going about things with their maids. He regretted firing them, because now he had questions to ask Mariana. He was sure she knew something. But she seemed to have disappeared. Not even her sister in Gamboa could locate her.

"And you mean to tell me you went looking for her on your own?"

"With no luck, however."

"But really, why do that?"

"Ms. Saxe, I feel I need to; I have to talk to Mariana. I think she knows more than she told the police about Silvia's death."

"Such as?"

"Whether it was entirely an accident!"

"You're uncomfortable, of course, in mourning."

"But more than that. There are facts I need to know."

"I can certainly understand," Vanessa said.

"So then: I know a few places where I thought it would be easy to find her--if she hasn't left Rio—so I just set out...Something is pushing me, compelling me, you could say."

After a moment Vanessa said, "Where did you think you would find her?"

"Ms. Saxe—if Mariana wasn't working for us she'd likely wind up on the street--hustling…"

"She's a prostitute—and nearly sixty?"

Said Dr. Roderigo, "Well, for the love of god, that woman doesn't look her age. I checked some awful places. You've heard of the Mangue?"

Vanessa had. It was a zone of pathetic whores who worked out of shacks, hidden on three sides behind a double-high wall of billboards. A fetid sewage canal eight meters across ran the entire length of the fourth side, forming a hard and stinking boundary with the everyday world.

"Awful—I've heard," said Vanessa. "Just what do you hope to find out?"

"I'm not sure," Dr. Roderigo said. "Sometimes when people get mixed up with macumba, they run into threatening criminals. I would like to know if something illegal happened to Silvia. Of course the police here never

wanted to take any time with the case. Accident suited them fine."

"What could be involved: drugs, or even murder?" Vanessa asked.

"Not impossible," said Dr. Roderigo, mulling over Vanessa's notion. "Something like that. I need to discover exactly what."

—

8.

Mariana leaned on her forearms while Geraldo plunged into her from behind.

"I once spent a whole week with an American...I fucked like a dog," she had told him down in the Erotika, to close their deal. You had to sell to get your trick...Finally, Geraldo achieved orgasm, exited, and flopped down at Mariana's side.

What happened to Silvia was an accident, or was it?

Back in July, on a cool morning, Dona Silvia and Ruth got into a taxi to do some shopping downtown.

Silvia stopped to ask Ruth, "Where are we?"

"Praca Tiradentes, Senhora."

After walking a few more blocks, Silvia wandered over to window-shop. There were books there: *A Guide to the Spirits, The Four Ritual Points of Umbanda, Kardec the Prophet.* According to a small sign, the four ritual points of umbanda were success, happiness, riches, and health.

Dona Silvia had just one.

"If she had gone for the tests Dr. Roderigo wanted, could she have had a child?" the john asked.

"Maybe so," answered Mariana, "I can't say for certain."

Inside the macumba shop Silvia wandered among shelves holding rows of plain and scented candles, more books, and there were feathered headdresses for Ogun, red pitchforks, plaster statues of the Virgin and of St. George, even a painting of Iemanja looking glorious in her sea-blue, sequined wardrobe, coming toward the beach at New Year's. There were drawers of herbal medicines and small metal statuettes of Exu.

Silvia whispered to Ruth.

"Leave it to me, senhora." Ruth turned to the shop attendant. "Can we have three of those candles—and two of these?"

"Look at this wonderful little perfumed soap, Ruth: *The Dream of Nymphs…*"

"Beautiful, senhora."

"One of those too, shop girl," said Silvia. "Is that all we need, Ruth?"

"A few more things."

"Wrap it up nicely please, missy, won't you?"

Now Geraldo rested atop Mariana, fastened to her ripe lower lip. As Mariana responded, returning the kiss, he felt himself tread water down, down to a depth where water became blood, and his heart went weightless, drifting like a sea-creature in a warm undercurrent.

Someone knocked at the door and opened it a crack.

The two love makers lifted up from their mattress. Mariana drew a sheet about her, tucked it between her bosom and shoulders, and went to answer. The man was still at sea.

Two of Mariana's girlfriends were at the door, peering in with interest, checking out Mariana's trick. Gossip darted between them like scavenging birds. The police were looking for her.

—

'So that's it," she thought. "He's got them looking for me."

Said Geraldo, "What's up?"

"No problem lover."

"Come on back here, come back to me, luscious. I can't get enough…"

Mister never could. Like that bastard, Dr. Roderigo.

But there came a day when he didn't want it with Dona Silvia anymore. Obviously, there wasn't going to be any child.

Dona Silvia grabbed the candles from her bedside table drawer, and then assembled the other things they'd bought downtown and went with Ruth to see a macumbeira called Dona Lucia. There were several women waiting there, in the green wallpapered living room. One of them reminded Silvia and Ruth to take off their shoes.

Silvia was almost too nervous to do it.

"Don't worry," Ruth whispered to her, "She's going to tell you how to use those things we brought."

"And that coffee you told me about?"

"She might recommend that."

Silvia worked her feet back into her shoes and got up to leave.

"No," Ruth told her. "That will ruin it with the macumbeira. You'll never be able to come here for a work again."

It was their turn. The macumbeira let Ruth come into her bedroom too, since Silvia insisted. Dona Lucia reclined on her bed. She wore a yellow dress with many white petticoats underneath and had an orange scarf wrapped into a turban securing her braided brown hair. She smoked a fat stogie, making huge quantities of smoke. She waved her hands around.

Dona Lucia knew what Silvia needed, since Ruth had told her when she arranged the meeting.

"Twenty-five bucks," was the first thing the macumbeira said. "Sit down on this bed, the two of you."

Silvia handed over the money and laid out all the stuff they'd bought in the Praca Tiradentes: the clay doll, toilet soap, tiny china animals, and candles. The macumbeira let Ruth light the candles. She put the rest of the stuff into a shoebox, and had Silvia hold that on her lap.

Dona Lucia got up from the bed and began to move around her bedroom, trembling and shivering. She'd pull the cigar from her mouth and spit into a bucket.

She came over to Silvia and blew cigar smoke straight into her face. Then she began to fashion the smoke around Silvia's body, sculpting the grey air with her palms.

Silvia nearly fainted.

"Don't worry," Ruth told her. "It's going very well."

Dona Lucia began to shake violently. She went down to the floor like a dog and started rolling over and back. She laughed hysterically, wildly. The gods were down there with her!

—

The macumbeira got up from the floor. She pointed her finger at Silvia.

"You're confused," she said. Her voice was the croak of a frog, a dog's bark.

"Grab those ribbons—those--over on my nightstand!"

The macumbeira took the cigar out of her mouth and burned through one of the ribbons. She opened the shoebox and threw the burnt pieces in.

"We'll be done with your confusion—just like that!"

"I don't feel confused...I know what I want."

"Dona Silvia, please—don't talk that way to Dona Lucia," said Ruth.

"Tudo bem, OK," growled Dona Lucia. "For the baby. That coffee...Ruth knows."

"But—my husband..." Silvia began.

"Say nothing more to me!" the macumbeira commanded.

"I have to ask you, what should I do with this box of pretty things? That wonderful soap."

"Keep it until you think you are carrying a baby. Then give it Iemanja, hand it over to the sea. Now, get out of here, fast, quick!"

Ruth bowed on the way out of Dona Lucia's bedroom, while the macumbeira laughed with the sound of a lewd old grouch...

"Yes, yes madam," Dona Silvia said, grabbing the special box. Only now she was no longer was a citizen of this world, poor thing.

9.

Brazilian Special Security Forces Report, Jan. 3, interview transcript of Mel Androu, street vendor

Lissen here: I liked that Vanessa but she worked in some crapola office, like twenty floors up in a big tower. They made me wait in the lobby first.

One gente fina in a business suit was clapping another on the back. The foreigner could speak Portuguese, and he embraced the Brazilian as he had learned we do when a deal is done.

"It's an honor to serve your prestigious firm, sir."

"Thanks. We're hoping Colonel Santos will be feeling better soon…"

"Yes, exactly. And the best to your lovely wife."

"Please come and visit us at the Yacht Club some time."

It was like that. Yes, Sir Asshole! It turned out to be a good thing I had put on my best clothes and gotten my second-best shoes shined. Otherwise, they never would've let me go up.

So, ya know, this tomfoolery was what happened high up in the office towers, where they made the big wide world flat again, into paper, I thought.

—

First Vanessa showed me her office. She had a big map of Brazil with different colored pins stuck in it, mostly around the large cities. Sao Paolo. Brasilia. Rio. Campo Grande. She was treating me right.

"Let me explain--I manage personnel for Bright and Peters, Mel," said the redhead. "My work involves interviewing new hires, planning assignments and tracking the performance of our employees throughout the country."

"Is that right, Miss? So—that map…"

"Spot on."

"But what do your pinheads do?"

"Professional staff, Mel. And what we do is to count other peoples' money. Actually, we check up on the people who count other people's money."

Now, Red in that room with the map of Brazil and the colored pins, it seemed like some kind of joke to me, school play. Piles of money for this mess?

But my aunt, who raised me, trained me to have good manners, so I said, "Then you're responsible for all of that? Impressive."

"Yes. I get a very good salary for what I do, and I often travel for work. I've been able to see a lot of Brazil: Recife, Fortaleza, Florianopolis, and Manaus."

"Right you are; you are lucky Miss. Our beautiful Brazil--that's a handful."

"Yes, I've met many excellent people as well. Not so bad for a young woman of 29 years, don't you think?"

"You live large, Miss. But what about that boyfriend of yours—that gente fina butt hole from the delegacia; what does he offer a cool and smart-looking Englishwoman such as yourself?"

You know detective, I could have used a lot of different words. You saw her, after all. Find me a Brazilian man…

OK then.

Vanessa laughed. "I wouldn't call him a boyfriend, or a butt hole, Mel. I met Dr. Roderigo when he came for a job here."

Count me out there for a worker in your company, I told her.

"Right, quite the joke," she said. "Seriously, though. Dr. Roderigo—he's a very good psychiatrist—together we were looking for someone at the ceremony that night. A woman who worked in his household until recently, named Mariana."

"And why didn't the great doctor hire a regulation private eye?"

"He wanted to talk to her himself. I know what you mean, but mind you, I also wanted very badly to see what a macumba ceremony was like. So I sort of steered him to hold off on the p.i."

"So, clever you are, Miss. And besides you're a little interested in Brazilian macumba—so you told me. How did Senhor Doc get the idea that this Mariana woman would be at that spot?"

—

"Another maid from Dr. Roderigo's household told him it might be a good place to look."

Then she told me the whole story, about Dona Silvia wanting to have a child, and finally getting involved with the macumbeiras. How Silvia took leave of our glorious planet, once and forever.

"I get it; somebody doesn't think Dona Silvia's death was an accident."

Red looked at me funny, so I guess maybe she had added up her situation and this resulted in a new sum.

"It's my job to investigate people who come to Bright and Peters for work, remember? And, for some reason, I find this Dr. Roderigo story exceptionally fascinating, Mel. So help me, I'm not sure just why I should feel this curious about the whole affair. That's why I thought you might be able to assist me."

Exceptionally fascinating? I saw she had done a mouthful of thinking. I said, "Me? Help you do what?"

"I thought that since you were at that location in the Estrada Sta. Marinha, you might know some people. You might know something special. You might be able to help find Mariana."

"I'm not helping that head-shrinking, spec-wearing gente fina medicine man."

"No—Mel, let's say that you'd be helping me."

10.

From the wide window of the Sonhos restaurant and bar on the Hotel Meridien's 35th floor Vanessa Saxe could overlook the night scenery of Copacabana, then Ipanema and see as far as Leblon. The coastline sprawled languidly toward the southwest like a recumbent and naked, bejeweled maja. Moving along the seaside avenues, traffic suggested a pointillist bloodstream. But it was the body itself, made of the barely visible masses of the sudden hills with night fogs steaming around them that really made the scene. Although the view typically was said to represent a reclining man, Vanessa, seeing it softened by nighttime Atlantic emanations, was certain that the South Zone of Rio actually resembled the dark body of a woman, busy with allure, alive and moving with flash jewelry.

Vanessa had been impressed by the fact that Dr. Roderigo was trying to find Mariana himself. She was curious about what the woman might say. A Friday night drink at 7 pm ought to be a fine time for her to find out more, and to make up her mind regarding Dr. Roderigo's application to Bright and Peters.

Now she sipped a frosty caipirinha, wondering whether, if she were to stay in Brazil much longer, she could remain as she had been—now that she considered it—somewhat protected and aloof. Sail, surf and sun would always be wonderful. Her boyfriend Alvaro Fontes had been a fantastic magazine centerfold dream. What a fool she had been, not to accept his proposal. What was wrong with her?

Could there be more for her in Brazil, more than a playground for the well to do and their foreign partner? There was a life on the ground, on the street. Did she want to be forever separated from that?

Dr. Roderigo entered the Meridien Bar. A gold medallion hung at his neck. Vanessa waved to him from a corner table.

—

"Good evening, Miss Saxe," he said. "It's very kind of you to suggest a place I could walk to from my new flat."

"Yes, I can be very considerate," said Vanessa. "This was one of my boyfriend's favorite spots. I did tell you about Alvaro Fontes?"

"I know the family." Dr. Roderigo's caipirinha arrived and they toasted: "chin-chin."

Dr. Roderigo followed the trail of Alvaro Fontes, asking Vanessa, "You still regret the way that happened…?"

"I was convinced I was right to ask for more time. Maybe in that way, I decided for myself, for my freedom. But I was surprised by their extreme response. I suppose I wounded their pride?"

"I'm sure you're right about that. And I'm sorry. But I suppose that is over, as you say."

"I'm afraid so."

"Now, Ms. Saxe, I was glad you called, because I feel I have to elaborate on something for you; if you don't mind."

"Yes?"

"Then—I'm sure you must know that under normal circumstances a man like me would never go to such a place as the Mangue? I went there looking for Mariana."

"Of course, I understand that—another sort of place, then?"

"Please, Miss Saxe, don't pull my leg. Now is not the time."

"I'm sorry." Vanessa looked past Dr. Roderigo, and out through the Meridien bar's immense windows. Somehow, she imagined she saw the doctor's face, or one very much like it, pressed up hugely against the plate glass from outside. This face peered suspiciously into the swank bar. Beyond the translucent visage, the sea swelled and rolled.

"Miss Saxe," Dr. Roderigo said, and he repeated, "---Miss Saxe, are you also curious about what Mariana might tell me?"

"By now I'm strangely fascinated, to be honest with you."

"Meanwhile, you didn't believe a word of what the fishermen told your Swede in Buzios?"

Vanessa shook her head no.

"Then why did you feel so bad about it, if you discredited it?"

Vanessa chuckled. "I suppose I felt bad because I discredited it! Then it wouldn't be a ghastly tall tale, but the truth. As it was, it only felt like more of my hard luck these days. What a careless and flimsy excuse to give to an adventurous woman."

"Yes, we don't believe in castrating sea monsters, do we, Ms. Saxe?"

"Rubbish. Nor in lighting candles and handing our fate over to a pack of demons, Dr. Roderigo."

"Yes, aren't we sensible, scientific?"

—

"As you know, I've always considered myself a thinking person, doctor."

"I like that. I have met many beautiful and also intelligent Brazilian ladies, but naturally, your style is different."

"I'll take that as a compliment. I could use a compliment right now."

"Then, let me offer to buy you dinner here."

"I would really enjoy that, Dr. Roderigo. I ought to let you know that I have a friend's party to go to in Ipanema after 10:30."

"Tudo bem, let's get menus."

They spent the meal explaining themselves more fully to one another. The subject of Mariana was not mentioned again until coffee came, well past 9:30.

"I would like to ask you a favor, Ms. Saxe. But perhaps you will enjoy it. Ruth told me about a ceremony where I might be able to find Mariana. I was hoping you could go there with me."

"When?"

"Sunday night, beginning just after sundown."

Vanessa needed no more encouragement. She said, "Then I will."

"It might be a little dangerous, Ms. Saxe. The Estrada Sta. Marinha is not a place where people like us normally go."

And I had never been cheated out of a blonde hunk by homen marihno before last Friday, thought Vanessa Saxe.

11.

"Look here, Mariana," said Geraldo, "You don't believe in all that macumba garbage, do you?"

"What does it matter to you?"

"Tell me. Tell the truth."

"The only thing that matters is not winding up behind bars."

'Entrar end cana? Why should she talk about jail?' Geraldo asked himself. Was she wanted for something?

"Dona Silvia went through with it, you see. Coffee and all. Ruth and Dona Silvia, yeah. What a team. But it was me that lost a job."

"Doesn't seem fair."

"It was like this. A week and two months after she first visited the cigar chomper, Dona Lucia Santos of Copacabana, Dona Silvia still had the damn box with those odds and ends destined for Iemanja sitting on the floor of her closet. The happy occasion of her pregnancy was not in sight. Dr. Roderigo had drunk the special coffee for days. More arguments and more tears. 'Soon we'll be lucky, love,' she told Dr. Roderigo.

"She started spending half the day on the phone talking with friends about it. A few of those fancy fools who can't even open a can of soup would come over and offer their excellent advice: 'Fire Ruth!' 'You're spoiling a nice nightgown.' 'Fire Mariana!' 'You didn't have your legs crossed at the macumbeira's, did you?'

"Her friend Leila Samantha Lopes had a better idea: 'Visit my fortune teller, Dona Elisabete do Carvalho, she's unbelievable, terrific.'

"'I can't see another one of those women!'"

But Silvinha did go.

Dona Elisabete led her to the terrace. Out there a heavy-set blonde lady was sunbathing in a bikini.

"For the love of God, Dona Elisabete, what about my privacy!" said Silvia.

"Please don't be concerned about Marcia," Dona Elisabete reassured her. "She is completely devoted to me. Ever since I told her that her little poodle Fofinha would never get well until Marcia stopped attending those horrible ceremonies Dom Ademar Souza holds near Largo do Machado...such a dirty place!"

"Ay—what happens there?"

"You don't even want to know. It is mainly a bunch of gays, bichas--you see."

"And?"

"Don't make me tell you—we hear stories about how those bichas have filthy orgies, right in the terreiro! Where everything should be pure."

"For the love of God! And how did Dona Marcia get involved?"

"Well, since her husband passed away, it has been just her and little Fofinha. When the poodle got sick, the bichas were so nice to her there...But don't you worry about all that, Dona Silvia. Leila told me all about you, and I have good news. Did you bring the donation?"

Silvia handed over $150.

"Hey, this Dona Elisabete was a sharp one, huh Mariana?" said Geraldo.

"Exactamente."

Out on Elisabete's sunny patio, Dona Marcia rolled over. She began to snore. Dona Silvia imagined Fofinha must be healthy again.

"You brought the things I asked you for?" said Elisabete.

"Of course."

Elisabete spread out the cloth of true fortune Silvia had, and lit candles at the four corners. She made a devotion and gazed with intensity at the center of the cloth. Then she stood up and walked around the patio, always keeping her right hand on a wall or the screen door.

"Now, here's what I have discovered. You have a powerful adversary..."

"Who?"

"We don't know who it is for sure."

"Ay, Dona Elisabete...Iemanja will never bless me!"

—

"Please don't say that, Dona Silvia. I told you I have good news. What I have found out is that Iemanja blesses the offspring of Dr. Roderigo de Moraes! Isn't that wonderful?"

Silvia sighed. "Yes, yes, thank you, we will be blessed, just so. But--my adversary...?"

"That person has temporarily closed your path to Iemanja, my dear."

"What person?"

"Someone who works in your home."

"Not Ruth!"

"No, it is the other one. She has had relations with your husband. She calls upon Exu Pagao to widen the rift between you and Dr. Roderigo."

"Mariana! I knew it."

"That wasn't true, was it?" asked Geraldo.

"I had told her not to visit Dona Elisabete," Mariana answered. "So now she didn't trust me."

"What can we do?" said Silvia.

"Dona Silvia, we will do a work to remove Exu Pagao from your lifelines. And you must send that woman Mariana away from your home immediately."

"Of course, Dona Elisabete. We'll get rid of her tonight."

"It wasn't true?" asked the john. "You didn't sleep with Roderigo?"

"How would such an event occur? But it gave Silvinha an answer. She went straight home to Dr. Roderigo, told him about the blessing on his children, and said I had to go."

"I slept with *her*!" Dr. Roderigo said, "That's absolutely ridiculous. You should know better, Silvia dear."

But now Dona Silvia was full of fire. "Ridiculous, is it? I'm not so sure, Roderigo. Meanwhile it's time for us to throw that black whore out! Should you be next!"

"Please relax yourself, Silvia—we can send Mariana away, no problem. But I'm not moving an inch. Can you

imagine…me? Focus yourself on the good part of what that fortune teller said."

"I served them dinner that night. Afterward Silvia picked a fight with me about forgetting the cream for her coffee. 'I think Ruth left it off the tray,' I said. 'Ruth, always blaming Ruth,' Dona Silvia yelled. She had a strange gleam in her eye.

"'I have no problem serving a good cup of coffee,' I told Dr. Roderigo. 'It's your wife and Ruth who are confused.'"

"'What nerve!'" Silvia shrieked. "'I won't stand for this.'"

"And that was that. I had to pack up and out I went. I felt like telling Dr. Roderigo everything: That he had been drinking a mixture of green leaves and his wife's menstrual blood with his coffee for weeks…But what difference would it have made? 'My poor, dear wife Sylvia mixed up with those things?' That's all he would have said."

—

"Gente fina really are the biggest lunatics, isn't that so?" Geraldo observed.

12.

Brazilian Special Security Forces Report, Jan. 3, interview with Mel Androu, street vendor

I didn't have a drop of luck finding that Mariana. So I called Vanessa Saxe. She told me to meet her outside her apartment building in Leme late that night. She asked me to bring a couple of my little Exus to show her friends, since we'd be going to a party.

She came down late, looking good in tight jeans and a man's white business shirt with a little silver tie. She had been talking on the phone to Dr. Roderigo, she said.

"Ass-face again!"

"Enough, Mel. It's his situation, after all."

"He can go back to the whore that made him!"

"Enough! What's the matter with you men? Please mind your manners, like you usually do."

I didn't have an easy answer for that. She said it was across town, where we were going, so we jumped into a taxi. To improve the mood, I showed her one of my wire gentlemen.

"Where are we going?" I asked.

"Nicely made little devil," she said.

"You need to know that Exu is not the devil, Miss. He is the imp of the crossroads. You have to satisfy this little bastard—(he and I are very similar in that way, sir)--so that he will open the paths."

"Oh, I see, Mel. Now, we're going to introduce both of you boys to some of my friends…and you can explain Exu then. By the way, what happens after the paths are opened?"

"Then? Then you can get a boatload of work done."

"I see. Mel, let me ask you this…do you think macumba is used more for good, or for evil?"

"Depends."

"Seriously."

"I'm talking serious. If a man wants to get away from his woman, and the lady gets a work done to hold him—is that good or bad? If a worker asks the gods to make a boss that abused him and then fired him suffer with a month of migraine headaches—or from a toe that suddenly falls off in the shower, what do you say? Good? Bad?"

She thought it over. "That's assuming it works…"

"Whatever, Miss. Not all of the time."

"And how do people go about it, when they want to do harm?"

"Ah, that's deep. You need to find a practitioner of quimbanda. They are the ones who can do it."

"Is it hard to find somebody like that?"

—

I told her that most practitioners do not enter the line of harmful magic. It is extremely dangerous work.

"You mean it gets out of control."

"Happens, Miss."

"How would a guy go about harming his boss?"

"First, the quimbandista would have to accept the work. Then the man pays for an animal sacrifice, like a goat…"

"A blood sacrifice."

"The goat dies. And the one who wants the work pays for cloth and thread and rice and dende oil and whatever else is requested."

"It could be expensive."

"Depends…sometimes the quimbandista does the work without receiving any fee."

"Really?"

"They are priests, remember?"

"If you think so…and what else?"

"They may take a small model of the boss and break its back or hang it upside down so that the boss will go bankrupt when his money falls out of his pockets—the practice they decide will work. After they make their offering, they put the model in a box and hide it on the enemy's turf. Or they put it somewhere he will pass by every day."

"And of course this does the trick."

"Oh, Miss, please--it can be effective. Not every time. I know many cases."

"That can involve criminal acts, Mel."

"You said it. Guys will usually make an offering before they go off to knock over a bank."

"Knock over a bank—that's plain theft…But your macumba could be used to kill!"

"Quimbanda. But they say that only men, diseases and natural causes kill people, Vanessa. You were asking about good or evil? Now I say: it's more often used for good. Our Brazilian people need so much help. Macumbeiras have performed miraculous cures. The priests are highly respected."

"And you believe in those cures? Don't you think the results they asked for could have happened anyway?"

"Doesn't stop people from praying in the Catholic Church. You don't do that, do you, Miss?"

"I'm not Catholic, Mel. And you're right, I don't attend church. But I believe in one sole God."

"Me, I depend on me," I told her. "But that doesn't mean I can't believe spirits are at work behind the curtain."

"I have to admit, I like the idea of possession. About receiving a spirit and dancing wildly, freed from what weighs you down. But the idea that actual work can be done by spirits? Forget about it until you show me a clear case."

"It's not just an idea. The saints are effective because they connect with the forces of nature. They are reality. How else do you explain what happened to Dona Silvia?"

"A desperate and infertile woman was hit by a car because her mind wandered while she was crossing the street. Doesn't that take care of it?"

"OK, wrap it up your way. Someone might have wanted her out of the way, right? But if you're so sure, why should we look for Mariana?"

Vanessa smiled. "It's very interesting. But why would anyone want to kill Silvia? I'm simply fascinated to find out how far it goes," she told me.

"Watch out—you're under the influence," Ms. Redhead.

"Sure, Mel. Not much else makes sense!"

We had arrived at her friend Richard's place in Ipanema. A bunch of mindless teenage gente fina hung out on the street corner there. Known as the smart set, they're totally useless.

With Red I got into the building a different way from my usual: the front door. Her friend Richard lived in one of those duplex penthouses. Boy, was this guy stuffed with cash! I bet he saw more grana in a day than I could bring in during twenty lives.

On the entry level of his place was a single large room with a beautifully buffed wooden floor totally bare of furniture. They were using it for dancing; it had some colored lights circling. It was mostly boys dancing there. We climbed a marble stairway. The second floor was the living quarters. From there a stairway circled up to a rooftop patio where Richard had a very small swimming pool.

Right away you could see this Richard was another bicha, who fucked boys. I don't know about you, detective, but I don't like bichas too much. I mean, each to his own, whatever, but I have never been able to stop myself from saying a few nasty things where that strange type is concerned.

Richard was an extremely powerful person in their firm, Vanessa told me.

All the guests sitting around the pool spoke English. Richard made a sign so his maid could bring out another pitcher of their "most powerful" lemon batida punch, so Vanessa and your great friend Mel Androu could join in the drinking. Batida mais poderosa, funny.

She kindly introduced me as a vendor of 'ritual items,' and they asked whether I worked right on the street

and what I had in my bag. To be honest, not one spoke our beautiful Brazilian language half as well as Vanessa. They were comfortable in their little English-speaking- person sector.

"What are they saying?" I asked.

"They want to see your Exus."

"You'll help me explain?"

"Carry on."

I lined up three little gentlemen on the glass-topped patio table, but nobody did more than look carelessly over our way. Vanessa said a few kind words. The English didn't stop their drinking; they were laughing and shooting off their traps. Vanessa invited them but nobody wanted to touch my little men.

—

"So they think it's funny?"

Vanessa heard my loud remark. "No, no—they're laughing at each other's jokes, that's all."

"I don't know...I bet these tipsy gringos are chicken!" I slammed a palm down onto the glass poolside table.

"Take it easy, Mel."

"I'm not a clown, Vanessa, to entertain these gente fina with my funny little men. Ask them why they don't care to take a closer look."

A wacked out Brazilian burst onto the scene. He was wearing a green shirt illustrated with yellow palms and

crocodiles. He had on no more clothes. It was another crazy bicha—Richard's loud-mouthed play toy.

"'Who is this ruffian?' he said, noticing me instantly. 'Mel Androu da Gamboa,' I answered. 'And those cute little Exus belong to you, I suppose, sweetheart?' 'Sweetheart my butt! Yeah, I make them, you—'"

Vanessa gave me a sharp poke.

All of a sudden, that crazy bicha yanked off his print shirt and splashed into the pool. Right away he started pretending to be drowning and splashed around wildly with his light-skinned twiggy arms. After that he commenced making silly noises, calling for Richard to join him over in the cabana.

"Vamos la, Ricardo," he yelled. "Agora mesmo."

Richard was quite drunk. "I can see your new boyfriend is a lot nicer than that hunk of Swede at Buzios," he said loudly to Vanessa. "He was good for *nothing*."

"That's enough, for Heaven's sake," Vanessa said to him.

The crazy bicha started jumping up and down, naked on the rooftop. He was pretending that what Richard had said about the Swede made him jealous. He was going to jump off the building and land on the cobblestones. What a pack of blowhards!

The bicha sat down next to me on the couch not using his towel and dripping wet. I shoved myself against Vanessa, who slid away.

The bicha said to me, "We Brazilians sure are suffering around here tonight, huh boyfriend?"

"Shut your face, you crazy, crappy bicha," I told him.

"Don't count on getting it on with her, handsome, you're as close now as you're gonna get," he said.

"The way you go from one to another, maybe it is magic, sweet," that drunk Richard shouted to Vanessa. He began pulling the crazy bicha back toward the cabana.

What fine folks!

Gente fina, indeed.

"All in fun," Vanessa said to me.

"Like a whore getting an abortion in the maternity hospital—of course!"

—

Another British guy, named Hilton, came up the circular stairway. He whispered something to Vanessa. He stank of rum.

"What's the matter?" I asked.

Hilton told her they'd said, "Your conduct is being discussed at the office. You are not in the business of researching black magic or irrelevant faith-healing."

"Well, good on it, then! The hell with them." She shouted in Hilton's face, so he moved away.

The Vanessa turned to me. She told me I'd better go. Cold. Now. Just like that! 'Get out.'

Sir, that was when I made up my mind.

13.

'Just remember,' began a learning mantra that Vanessa repeated aloud in her flat as she waited for Dr. Roderigo to collect her on Sunday afternoon: 'the goddess of the sea is the Virgin. The virgin is the Goddess of the Sea.'

The sun was setting beyond Morro da Gavea when Dr. Roderigo's Mustang entered the just-finished Tunnel Dois Irmaos. By the time they were out of the long tunnel, heading up the Estrada Sta. Marinha, he had turned off his headlamps.

Now you could hear the drums warming up. The big bass bottoms were frightening voices from the spirits' basement.

Ragged people shied from the light as the Mustang moved down the lane. The clearing was large, and the forest sloped gently upward on the far side. Beyond that, the lump of the Morro da Gavea rose abruptly. In the middle of the clearing, three tall trees were all that remained standing above the bare ground, packed hard over time by the many dancers who had come sincerely seeking a nourishing connection with Mother Earth via their chosen saints.

There were just a few light bulbs hanging from wires.

People were already dancing. Big white skirts swirled. The loose-fitting blouses of the Bahianas had enormous sleeves edged with lace; many golden baubles and cheap black and green bead necklaces tangled and swayed, jangling against the big black wooden crosses they wore and clinking against their shining silver medallions.

They sang: "O meu Pai Xango, cura meu dor." Cure my pain, Father Xango!

Under the trees, the night was green and black in different patches. Full of nervous energy, Dr. Roderigo searched the shadows for Mariana.

The drums began to insist, reaching toward the bottom of everything. The women's voices rose to a high-pitched moan as they circled, dancing, seeking a partner. They seemed desperate to be with their gods.

Vanessa caught the awesome vibration. She knew this was it: macumba, voodoo, whatever you wanted. You could feel the awful power, and she *was* afraid.

Now one dancer broke into a stutter-step, falling at an angle toward the ground. Another woman staggered and

—

would have fallen over backwards if a dancer had not opened his arms to catch her.

Vanessa and Dr. Roderigo were ignored. There was no eye contact.

The feeling of separation irked Vanessa. She clutched Dr. Roderigo's arm tightly and he winced.

"They don't want us here," she said.

"Nobody's bothering us. Please don't hang on so tightly, Vanessa—I need to be able move around and find her."

"Right, doctor. Regardless, I have to say that I'm beginning to feel a little uncomfortable."

"Do you want us to go—?"

"Maybe, but not just yet. I'm afraid, but I like something here, too. I feel the vibrations of those drums travelling up through my thighs…"

Dr. Roderigo looked her over sideways.

Now they saw how angry eyes regarded them from dark, mask-like faces. No one said a word. Many more people had arrived, and around the dancers a lacey white circle of onlookers swayed. The drums took up a new, milder rhythm. Vanessa felt the beats come to rest in her panties.

The slowdown didn't last. Now that the clearing was filling there was a fresh flourish, and the drummers raced off, tempo thundering like Valhalla.

This sent the dancers in the circle into frenetic motion. Six or seven women began to stagger in response, to pitch and spin wildly, half-stumbling and looking as something had tossed them off a merry-go-round . One dove to the ground and flopped like a fish out of water. Another fell hard to her knees, looking like she hadn't felt a thing. She began to shake and pray.

Vanessa saw one Bahiana's eyes roll inward. Blank spaces seemed to gaze back at the world most people thought of as real. She was somewhere else.

The frenzied lurching and shaking of the dancers worked its way toward a unified whirlwind of white skirts, a gathering wind tornado.

Enraptured, Vanessa saw it an as attempt to rise out of earthly bondage. She felt the thrust rise up through the beaten earth.

"They look like epileptics," said Dr. Roderigo.

At first Vanessa didn't take it in, so the doctor repeated himself.

She said, "That's an ugly thought! Surely you can appreciate their dancing."

"I'm concentrating on something else. You know what we came for."

The white skirts were whirling, and the women begged: "O meu Pai Xango, cura meu dor." The dancers flung themselves into spiritual possession and found the half-beyond and the in-between.

It was nothing easy! It was so bloody intense!

—

"What do you suppose they are working toward?" Vanessa asked.

"I don't know," said Roderigo. "Remember, we don't believe in this."

Vanessa had surmised all along that he perceived the events of the last months mainly as an affront; his masculinity was wounded; he had been impatient for a child and was frustrated as his family dream went out of control. She also had been trying to assay what he saw in her, beside the job opportunity. Right now she sensed something twisted about the doctor's reaction to the ceremony in the Estrada Sta. Marinha. His denial.

'Why is it so important to be here, if only to track down Mariana?' she thought.

Vanessa knew how above-it-all certain Brazilians of the better classes felt, and like them, many of her English friends, living in a country where so much was unequal. The way it went, some pour souls still were no better than slaves. Vanessa enjoyed feeling above-it-all too, but not to appreciate the primal celebrations of others? Not to see the beauty in the clearing that ghastly night--that was trivial.

Meanwhile, to approach Brazil on the ground, where the whirling dancers were, this continued to give her pause. If one were to embrace that frenzied world of spirits, could one trust the consequences? How could a sea creature that assaulted a traveler's genitals be acting in anyone's better interest?

Vanessa looked around the circle, contemplating the arrangements of magic. It struck her that Dr. Roderigo, who was stalking about searching faces, wasn't going to find Mariana. She felt overheated, and she needed to calm down.

"Perhaps it's time for us to go," she suggested.

"Maybe that's a good idea, Vanessa. I'm not that happy about being here anymore. Same as you."

'Not quite,' she thought.

There were plenty of rough characters around. One smartly dressed, street-smart looking black guy in particular had been staring across the circle at her with purpose, meanwhile chain-smoking cigarettes. When she had a clear look, Vanessa was shocked: the man was much darker, but didn't he look something like a much younger Dr. Roderigo? She remembered this face, was sure she had seen it before: it was the face that pressed upon the windows at *Sonhos Bar* at the Hotel Meridien, coming into focus from out of the night fog.

Confusing. And yes, really it was menacing, the way the Bahianas' voices droned and whined and implored. One old gal was clunking about heavily, elephantine ankles ringed with twinkling silver bracelets dragged her white petticoats through the dirt. Out of her mouth came the brutal voice of a wolf.

Now the drums sounded with a hollow, metallic echo. In the faint light, Vanessa could make out reddish smears on the drum skins—at some ceremony the believers must have sacrificed to the drums as well! How strange!

'Beira mar ah way beira mar,' the women sang. It sounded like a reference to the sea.

Vanessa swayed to the beat.

—

The black guy had made his way around the circle and was trying to talk to Dr. Roderigo.

"What's he say?"

"Police!" the black guy shouted.

A hundred whistles blew. People ran off helter-skelter toward the forest that climbed the towering Morro da Gavea. Vanessa saw flashlight arcs cut through the frozen tableaux of the dancers who hesitated in formation as the drums stopped speaking.

Dr. Roderigo greeted the police officers as if they were doing him a favor.

14.

Fireworks thundered; it was well past 11 pm. Mariana lifted off the mattress to watch an early salvo: a golden design showered the sky. With that she relaxed. She crept back along the sheet to Geraldo's side, and gave him a wonderful kiss.

"You're OK, baby," she said to him, "we'll welcome the New Year together."

"That's the spirit!"

He began to lick between Mariana's legs.

"That feels good," she said, after a while, "but it's enough."

"I could stay there forever."

"You're a regular lion, Mr. Geraldo. What do you do with the rest of your time?"

"I'm an electrician."

"Bless you, honey. Brazil needs electricity."

"Yeah. So, Mariana—what happened to the de Moraes after you left their service; did you find out?"

"Sure, I stopped by a couple of times and met Ruth in the park...She told me that one afternoon, she found Dona Silvia sitting on the floor in front of her big closet. She had her wedding dress out of its box. She was pulling at the material and sobbing."

"Poor thing."

Silva still had the shoebox of things that Dona Lucia prepared for her hidden in her oversized closet.

"What are you doing, Dona Silvia?"

"Leave me in peace, Ruth..."

"But."

"I'm throwing all this out," Silvia said.

"Dona Silvia, for the love of God!"

"Go away, Ruth, just go away."

Silvia was desperate. She went by herself to consult with Dona Lucia again. The macumbeira's look frightened poor Dona Silvinha.

"You've ruined everything," Lucia told Silvia. "I shouldn't talk to you!"

—

"Please, Dona Lucia."

"Your lack of faith sends you every which way," said the macumbeira. Ruth had told her about Dona Elisabete, the fortuneteller. She was offended.

"Look me in the eye, Dona Silvia. What do you really want?"

Sylvia still wanted a baby.

"Then take the box we fashioned…"

"And what, Dona Lucia? What should I do with it?"

"Oh—I really don't want any more of you! I've had my fill!"

"Please, I'm begging, Dona Lucia! God help me!"

"That's right: beg. Go--write a message with your wishes to Iemanja and place that into the box with the rest. Give it to the sea. Now, get out of here. And do what I told you, quick!"

Sylvia paid her money. She took the box to Copa and watched it bob in the waves. But she would never conceive.

Not that it's so hard for some of us, Mariana thought. I'm just the god-damned soul of fertility! She had a few children out there. Years before, in Minas, her very first boss had given her a son; he demanded she serve him one afternoon at the family's country house. She was thirteen. When Mariana refused, he called one of his gardeners in and the guy brandished his machete while de Moraes raped her. Only you didn't call that rape; it was accepted in Brazil.

The great man later sent his boy to be raised in his own brother's home. Mariana was sent there to work as well, but she never told the boy that he was her son.

Thirteen years later that uncle sent that very boy, who he'd raised as his own, to learn the arts of love from Mariana in her tiny servant's room. There was nothing Mariana could do to escape the scene. Her own son! This time when she became pregnant, she was handed a few bucks and shown the door. Wouldn't do to let the boy have an inkling that he'd had a child with that maid. She made her way to Rio and gave birth.

Soon afterward Mariana began to unravel and could barely take care of herself. Finally she went missing. Her sister raised the baby in Gamboa. She had only met him a few times over the years, and the aunt had never told the boy that Mariana, a visitor passing through, was his mother.

If only Dona Silvia would have had such problems!

"So Geraldo, acting upon the macumbeira's orders, Silvia wrote a note begging for a child, cried over it, enclosed it in the box, knelt at the water's edge, prayed, and launched it to Iemanja."

She waited another month. Dr. Roderigo was finding it difficult to be around her; he suggested she spend some days living at her mother's. Silvia was crushed. How could she have a child when she was no longer living with her husband! Was there that much magic?

But her mother just egged Dona Sylvia on. "Darling, you and I know for certain that he slept with that street tramp Mariana. After all he's done, you should leave him forever."

—

"No, Mama, Roderigo is a good husband. I really don't believe he did that!"

"Darling, just be thankful that the whore is out of your life."

"Ay, Mama, I can't live this way!"

"Somebody up there must have heard Dona Silvia," Mariana said to the john. "Because a couple of days later her life ended when she was crushed under the wheels of that car."

"For the love of god," said Geraldo, "You don't say!"

15.

Brazilian Special Security Forces Report, Jan 3, interview with Mel Androu, street vendor

Oh, come on friend! Enough fucking questions! Like I told you already: I did it! Nabbed her! It's not a bit complicated. I hate all those foreign gente fina! The way they treat us Brazilians. The people of this country, right here, you and me, good buddy!

What do you mean, you inspectors aren't sure? Let me finish what I've been telling you then....

So a few days after that party I showed up at Vanessa's place in Leme. She let me in, no questions asked. That surprised me. But Red was always bold.

She was sitting on the floor, wearing a pair of frayed-edge shorts and a tee shirt from the British football club Manchester United. The tee shirt was tight as a baby's butt and the curve was large, my brother. She was talking on the phone, arguing. I realized it was that horse's-ass, Dr. Roderigo de Moraes. Again! She motioned for me to sit down. The argument went on. She hung up hard.

"That's the limit," Vanessa said.

"What's up, now Miss?" I asked.

"Dr. Roderigo is giving up. He doesn't want to look for Mariana anymore. I think those three hours in the police station were more than he could tolerate. He'll accept the fact that Sylvia's death was an accident. While I've become convinced that there's more to it."

I felt the same way: there was something more and maybe she wasn't telling me. Her face showed so much discomfort; I saw Red was very frustrated, comrade. I understood how that could help my plan.

"What can we do?" I asked.

"Get on with it," she said. She looked at me directly and said another thing. "Let's get out of my apartment, Mel. I feel cooped up. Let's get outside and walk and see what we see. Then we'll have some ideas." She looked for some sandals and attached the straps over her long, lovely, tan-over-pink feet.

It was better than I planned. I felt a little sorry right then, for what I was planning. Vanessa was not in the slightest, friend, the worst of those fancy people. Oh, she started out on a high steed, of course. But, oh, no, no, not by far as bad as it gets. I'm sure you know what I mean. But that's the way it is: you only touch what you can reach.

—

We were out walking along Avenida Atlantica. Heavy traffic sped between the huge, patterned sidewalk and the wide beach. It was warm, with an oceanside breeze.

"He didn't even catch sight of Mariana?" I asked her.

"Let it go for a minute," she said.

"Look." I had thought it out. "It's this here," I told her. "From all you've said to me, I'm sure Mariana must have influence over Dr. Roderigo's family—a powerful influence. Somehow, by getting so interested and involved, you have caused that influence to extend to you."

"I refuse to consider it! I'm doing nothing more than studying these events."

"All good: If it was that way, you could forget everything right now. Go ahead, walk away. But I know you won't."

She gave that a thought.

"Let me show you something," I said.

"Show me what?"

"We can talk to a guy who knows more about evil works. We can find out if he knows something about Mariana's shady business. Or if he might have an idea about Silvia…"

"Dirty business, you mean. Now? You mean you want to go there right now?'

She wasn't a nervous type, but Vanessa seemed a little nervous.

I said, "You like the truth, isn't that what you told me, Miss? You 'get to the bottom of things.' I think you said that to me once or maybe even twice."

"Fine, Mel: I'm not feeling that fit, but let's keep walking. Maybe something in the fresh air will pick me up. You'll be delighted to find yourself with Vanessa Saxe, Rio's rising star."

We crossed Av. Atlantica at a stoplight and stepped into the cool sand to continue along Copacabana Beach. Vanessa started moving along like it was hard to walk. You know how it can be on sand. Then she stopped, took off her sandals, gulped a large breath and picked up the pace.

"See?" she said.

"No keeping you back, Miss!"

But you know, friend, I was heading for Dom Nelson's hillside place, over on the Morro do Cantagalo. He's a friend of my aunt, good people. Well, Nelson says he can receive Ogun, and here you go: no one ever has. Meanwhile, he's the type who's always saying he'll do anything for you. And why not, he's got nothing else to do. So he does anything!

Naturally, I'd set things up with him beforehand.

"How's your aunt—that miracle of womankind?" he asked me when I had climbed up his crappy hillside to lay out the action. "Not Ilma…"

I cut him, off. "Listen here, Dom Nelson, I don't have time for gossip."

—

We arranged what Ogun would tell Vanessa.

That evening, Vanessa and me--after strolling the beach for a while like a gente fina couple on parade--we headed back through the traffic and walked inland a few blocks toward the morro. She remembered to put her sandals back on and leaned against me. I sniffed the sweet air, but I was too busy steering, naturally. I bought her a cafezinho at a corner coffee stand. She set the empty cup down on the white tiles.

"Obrigado Mel, that perked me up."

Her light blue eyes started to shine again. We began climbing the mud-slippery steps toward the favela along with the rest of the pack animal human-beings. Old ladies carried tons of dirty gente fina undies wrapped into bundles on their heads—such a wonderful crown! Slim young babes

with nice brown ankles. Someone's butt swaying in your face. People began staring at us. Vanessa was a little worried, but I told her I guessed that all of the staring was because before that, no one with red hair had ever climbed up the Morro do Cantagalo. But I'd been in that kind of place plenty.

Courageous Red!

A rat slid down the water chute beside the steps.

We finally reached Nelson's: halfway up there, almost a hundred meters high. You could look down over the city backed by its darkened beaches, the waters of Guanabara Bay and the Atlantic. Black sky, dark hills, smell of the bay, stars out, lights of cars along the seaside run. Ocean. Vanessa. The smell of Vanessa coming and going with the breeze. Me.

"Oba—Uncle Nelson!"

The huge man made a fine start. He had on the perfect Ogun outfit: cardboard armor, red plumes, Saint George's big silver sword (made of cardboard and tinfoil). He had painted the crossed blades of the warrior Mars all over his legs and arms. He was an imposing dark man covered with ugly red moving tattoos.

"Bloody Hell!" Vanessa said when he jumped out of the backside of his shack onto the terrace, tottering.

"Respect!" Nelson sounded off, a brown bear with a toothache. Ogun was surely on his way!

The warrior took us a few steps downhill from his terrace to a little reddened stone firepit, located on a plateau right at the bottom of Nelson's Babylon Hanging Garden of

three tomato plants and sumptuous weeds. He snapped a chicken's neck that he had tied there. He slashed the bird, drawing blood.

"What's all this for?" asked Vanessa.

"He takes care of Exu."

"Silence! Absolute silence!" The warrior growled. He lit candles and placed them around the pit. The red crosses kept crawling around on his just about midnight-twenty skin. They don't come much blacker than Uncle.

"Silence!" Nelson's eyelids shut down. Then—this man I hired—I think he really did receive a spirit! He started shaking like a leaf. He waved his cardboard blade in the air like honest warfare. He opened his old man's eyes and looked out, surprised as shit.

—

"What do you two persons want?" moaned the warrior Ogun.

I said: "Sr. Ogun, we would like to know, if you would please tell us, that is, if you know if there were any works done against Dr. Roderigo de Moraes and his departed wife, Dona Silvia."

Then enormous Ogun stopped quivering. The tattoos froze.

"Who? —Oh yes, yes!" He laughed like a bear in a tv cartoon.

I said, "Evil works? That caused Dona Silvia's death?"

Dom Nelson had been prepared, but Ogun hesitated. The flimsy tinfoil-wrapped cardboard sword, barely moving now, bent candlelight. He scratched the wobbly point in the dirt.

"Listen here, Sr. Ogun!"

I couldn't believe it, because it looked like my useless uncle might actually fall asleep on his feet. He breathed heavily. The red plumes of his headdress bobbed between tomatoes.

I shouted: "Was Mariana responsible?"

The warrior banged his reddened fists on the low stone wall of the pit. His red plumes shook in the night air. The stars went away, came back. The god's mouth opened. An empty bubble escaped. He didn't say a thing.

"Tell us, please, sir," said Vanessa evenly.

Ogun shook his head: yes, no, yes.

"Maybe he means that she receives," I said. "Then it wouldn't really be her, but the will of a god. You understand, Vanessa, she wouldn't be at fault."

Ogun said nothing to that. So far, so good. Then it came out, like a disgusting burp. Who told that horse's-ass of a Nelson to invent?

"Mel Androu is a danger to you, Vanessa," said the big dummy in the cardboard armor, Nelson-Ogun. For you the guy would do anything, right?

Vanessa looked at me, your current prisoner Mel Androu.

"I suppose I should ask him what he means?" she questioned me.

The fat man mumbled. "He carries the seaweed health of homem marinho in his bloodstream. Out of the line of Iemanja," said Nelson.

Then he shook, burbled a little more and passed out drunk into the bloody firepit. His red feathered headdress garnished the decapitated chicken.

All right, I thought, show's over. I've failed.

Vanessa looked at Nelson lying there and frowned. She laughed a little.

"Whatever *that* means, I'm happy to find out for myself," she said.

I looked at her, controlling my astonishment. "I'm glad miss. Let's pay him something," I said.

—

"This guy deserves to be paid?" she joked.

I shook my head. As you wish. She took a little folded up cash from the pocket of her frayed- style short dungaree shorts and was ready to throw it onto the ground. People were going up and down the favela steps a few meters away.

I said, "Hold on here. I'll get his wife to come out and then we'll beat it. Don't worry, I'll be quick."

"Where to?" she asked.

"Up this way."

"Up? Yes, the answer's up there, I'm certain," she agreed and looked there. She tossed her red mane back over her shoulder with courage.

I motioned up the darkened hillside. Up there, you could barely make out trees bent over like rows of fringe.

She was gazing into the blackness, with blind eyes, so I pointed, "Up there." Seeing that she kept looking up the hill, I congratulated myself on my plan. You know how that goes, sir!

16.

All the while Vanessa and Mel climbed further up the steep Morro do Cantagalo, she felt as if she were actually going down. Every step up the difficult path was another step down. She had fallen to Earth and beyond. She would now engage the night in Rio de Janeiro and afterwards, perhaps, descend into Hell. What would make the difference about which direction she would go?

After twenty minutes climbing, they reached a clearing right beneath the tapering fringe top of the morro. They looked down. The city spread out below them, a million fireflies around its black lagoon.

"Where have you taken me, man?" Vanessa asked Mel. She was tired and an urge to relax was overwhelming her, as if she had taken a powerful narcotic. With this, she experienced a newfound willingness to surrender control.

"We're here. It's a place I stay sometimes."

'This is not me,' Vanessa thought. She did not let go of Mel's hand as he carefully led her around to the far side of the small hilltop flatland. There was darkness amidst the tangle of tall shrubs for them to negotiate. They reached a shack overgrown with vines.

Struggling with exhaustion and unfamiliar rapture, Vanessa composed herself and, gesturing at a clear view outward near the doorway said, "Mel, this is the most spectacular view of the city. It's the most wonderful sight I've *ever* seen."

"Cidade Maravilhosa," said Mel.

"Yes, of course. That's what we call it."

"You are just about Brazilian, Vanessa. Anyway, let's go get something to eat," said Mel Androu. Inside the shack he lit an oil lamp.

"I'm hungry, you're right," said Vanessa. "Now Mel, don't lie: you planned to bring me up here, didn't you?"

"You could say that."

—

"I've been kidnapped," Vanessa said gravely. "Actually, I don't mind."

On a kerosene ring, Mel warmed up some beans from a tin. They drank cachaca straight from a bottle.

"Very good," said Vanessa, when the meal was done. She yawned.

"You're tired?" he asked.

"Yes, considering one thing and another. We can sleep here, Mel, right?"

"That's right, Vanessa," he said.

Noticing that it was just the one dim room with one bed, Vanessa lay down.

"Come on Mel," she motioned to him. "Let's sleep." She went out like she expected to find all of her answers in a dream.

When Vanessa woke up in the morning, her arm was around Mel's shoulder. It felt very comfortable. She kissed him and they made love. Afterwards she realized that it had been nearly four months since she had broken up with Alvaro Fontes. Not so long since the Swede told her about being attacked by homen marinho. Now in the arms of a trinket vendor. Wonder Woman, she thought.

"That was quite nice, Mel," she said.

"I liked it too, honey. Almost too much. But there's something I need to tell you…"

"Shush," she said. "Let's just lie here peacefully. We deserve it."

Later, when they awoke again, he said, "Don't tell me you aren't thinking about what Ogun told us?"

"That you take bloody power from Homen Marinho and his blinking seaweed cloak, Mel? Sure it's phony, but after this refreshing sleep night and day it makes me feel that I must carry on, continue the risk of knowing you, and find out what really happened to Silvia de Moraes. I can't stop without understanding. I am determined and not tired or afraid. Although yes, it may endanger me."

"Tudo bem—very well. Phony or not, huh?"

They did not leave the bed often that day, and Vanessa could not remember another afternoon like that in her life. Now it was sunset, and as the Brazilians said, that would mean--Vanessa wasn't sure what day of the week it was–"Then it's sunrise tomorrow, all good?" She did not want to let Mel go far.

"So you think we'll locate that Mariana?" he asked her brusquely.

"If not, I don't think we can ever find out what happened to Silvia."

Half-heartedly, Mel agreed. He said, "I need to fix some food now or we won't have dinner."

Vanessa yawned. "Yeah mate, I am hungry," she said.

They woke up early on New Year's Eve day after a second night of blissful sleep. Vanessa sat at the little table

—

eating stale crackers, some tuna directly from a can and no mayonnaise. Surprisingly tasty.

"Tonight will be New Year's, Mel. Maybe it's the right time to go back down the hill and celebrate with some others," she said. "Or would we do better to stay here, lover?"

"Not until they bring me the money, Vanessa."

"The money? What money are you talking about?"

"What money? The money I asked your company to pay to set you free, Vanessa. The money I demanded in my ransom note. The money those safados owe me for treating me the way they have. The money they owe every black bastard in Brazil!"

"What locura, Mel!" said Vanessa, standing up stark naked. Her lovely breasts swayed. "Bonkers! You have to be kidding! My company won't pay anything to set me free. They've fired me!"

"No, you must be the crazy one, Vanessa. What idiot would fire a woman like you?"

Mel picked up an unloaded pistol from under the bed and waved it around. Meanwhile, he held his left hand out, as if saying, 'look at this piece of work,' while showing off Vanessa to leering plantation house buyers at a slave auction.

He announced, "Not a chance they let you go, Vanessa, you're just the one for any job!"

Mel sat at the table for a while with his head down and thought, 'What is the point?' He put the piece down, and slowly reviewed the gorgeous redheaded

Englishwoman. He could find no obvious flaw. Tall and stark naked, with endless legs and an orange-mahogany bush, she could have inflamed the desire of any guy until the end of whatever. So much for the slave auction.

He picked up his pants and went out of the shack. Vanessa didn't move.

"Just going out to take a piss," he said, but after several minutes Vanessa saw that he wasn't coming back.

17.

Mariana's mind raced. Silvia is dead, she thought, and here I am, with the police on my African tail. Well, I didn't kill anyone. But any moment those blue and grey bastards will blow down the door and spill into this room with their nightsticks raised. They'll throw this poor electrician up against the wall in his birthday suit. They'll be having a fine party with my black ass. I'll be lucky if I ever get booked.

"I beg you: I'm sure you have something to say to me now, Iemanja, mother?" she asked aloud.

"Mariana?" shouted Geraldo.

"Can you take me please?"

"Hey, beautiful…are you talking to me?" said Geraldo. He was creeping backwards on the mattress, away from Mariana.

Mariana shrieked, "When it's time, take me, Mother, please."

—

Pandemonium overtook the living city and penetrated the noisy, soul-dense environment of nighttime. Rockets smacked every which way into the firmament, showering sparks, shedding a weird light over things. Silvia had been dead less than three months. Someone named Vanessa was out there, but not with Dr. Roderigo de Moraes. People danced barefoot and set off sizzling fireworks on all the Rio beaches; the faithful crews made ready to launch Iemanja's incoming rafts. You heard deafening blasts, screams, cheers. And there was more, more than could be witnessed with the three-dimensional eye.

Soon Mariana was pinching Geraldo's stomach muscles as he came again. He felt her become less solid, floating in waves beneath him, towing his body gently, like a warm current in the sea. Then she seemed to fade and Geraldo became one with the calm. In a moment it would be midnight, and a fabulous New Year.

18.

Brazilian Special Security Forces Report, Jan 3, final interview with Mel Androu, street vendor, confessed to abduction

Friend, do you remember this story from the sixties? When the leftists captured that American ambassador here in Rio? People say they sat around the room, with the poor old asshole in a blindfold, having political discussions! It makes you laugh. They say the old fellow agreed with a lot of what those 'desperate lunatics' were talking about. With their 'communist propaganda'…

He knew they had to have something right! 'Cause the gente fina and their foreign friends are just using us poor folk as pack animals, isn't that so? The foreigners don't come here to help us!

No comment, huh, Senhor Inspector?

I never found out why the company let Vanessa go. Maybe it was because of that safado, Dr. Roderigo. Or because she showed up at that party with yours truly, this real-world son-of-a-bitch from Gamboa, Mel Androu. Somebody must have complained.

Poor Red!

After I left her, I made my way down Morro do Cantagalo. I knew I would have to leave town fast. Yet there was no way I could go without checking in with Auntie Ilma. I told her I might not be around again for a very long time.

"I need to know something," I said.

"What, son?"

"You have to tell me the truth, exactly that, Aunt Ilma."

"I understand."

"Aunt, I have met my mother, haven't I?"

"To tell the truth, yes. A couple of times. Do you remember that tall, fine-looking black lady who was here once or twice when you were a kid?"

"That Maria? Who used to leave those wonderful, scented candles with us every time she came by? That was my mother?"

—

"Don't you remember the wonderful spice cake she brought for your birthday--you must have been eight or nine?"

"Sure. We had such a nice party, Auntie."

Sir, deep inside I felt all soft then, and I wanted to cry. But the feeling was buried too far down. I needed to be on my way.

"So, it was that Maria, Aunt Ilma! It's hard to believe. If I could only see her one more time..."

"Mariana," my aunt said.

"What, Aunt Ilma?"

"To tell you the truth, her name is Mariana. She never called herself that anymore after she brought you here from Minas. After her crazy time, she always called herself Maria."

"Minas?" I said.

"Yes, son, you and your mother came here from Minas."

"Don't tell me, Aunt Ilma! You said my mother was a daughter of Iemanja, in awful deep?"

"All the way inside, that's true."

I had to sit down. "So all the stories you told me about my mother, about how I was born in the house of that lousy big shot in Minas, all this was about that Maria, Mariana?"

"Exactly that, son. She could never let you know that she was your mother—because of the shame that came with the way of having you."

I wrestled with the shock. That safado Dr. Roderigo was my father! My brother! But I couldn't believe that my mother would kill.

"I have to find her Auntie. Before I run. I have to warn her!"

"Warn her why?"

"Because of the cops. There's no time to explain. It's critical!"

My aunt had only one idea about where to look.

"In Praca Maua?"

"I'm afraid so, son."

"For the love of Christ, Aunt Ilma."

Right that moment I had to clear out. We embraced. I looked back once. She was crying.

You could hear her calling softly, "Be careful, son."

I went down the street. Firecrackers were being tossed off the hillsides. I knew it was the last day of the year. I wanted to talk to Mariana.

It was a crazy risk, but I had to try. I made my way downtown. I spoke to some working girls outside the Cowboy and the Scandinavia Bars and convinced them I needed to find Mariana.

—

They stopped me at the hotel reception desk. They wouldn't let me go up. I argued and tried to force my way up the stairs, but a burly bouncer grabbed me. That was it. They knew I was wanted and held me there. Local cops showed up. They handed me over to you guys without roughing me up too much. I never got to see Mariana. Midnight came and went and it was a new year.

So here I am. Behind bars again. A 'big operator' who sells 'little devils' on the street. I abducted Vanessa, right? Everybody gets a surprise. You as much as me.

No, not devil, not devil!

Foreigners!

I'm sorry sir; you have been very fair with me. You have listened to everything I've had to say.

I hope they never find Mariana. She wouldn't have killed Dona Silvia. That really must have been an accident, or was it—what do you think?

Can homen marinho hurt a Swede or make love with someone like Vanessa?

They never did find her, you say? When the cops burst in, she was gone? Just a poor john, in his birthday suit and half out of his wits with fright…?

I want to thank you, sir, for telling me this. We're done now, aren't we? There's nothing left for me to say. Perhaps you know more.

Oh, listen, one more thing, if you would be so kind: when we're on the way back to the local lock-up, could we stop for a minute? I need to get these black shoes shined.

Here, detective sir, you've been so kind, let me get the door. After you.

19.

New Year's: Fala Iemanja: Iemanja speaks:

"You are no more you.

Thousands, look at them, come to see me! Mariana that I was. Iemanja I am. I ride toward the beach on this, my lovely raft. I come to Copacabana Beach to bless the new year.

Look at all the candles. My lights of love!

The drums thunder. The beach sways. Whirls. People get dizzy.

Oh, my faithful, so many.

Come to my waves. Come to me! See my raft piled with glorious flowers: red, yellow, pink. Have no fear. See my beads, trailing blue like the sky. My turquoise dress has a train, like a path of moonlight on the shimmering sea. On my raft I come to all of you, bringing you a fragrant bouquet.

Black. Arms upraised. To embrace you with all of my heart.

I see your candles and I can hear your prayers. So many.

Sing to me. Oh, my darlings, what can it be?

—

Sailor, I do not own the sea, but I have come to save you.

Here I am, floating in. To feel your pains, to answer your prayers.

Candles! As if the night burned, all one flame.

Here they come. The Bahianas in white dresses sway. Into my waters they wade. Toss soft petals on my waves.

The city strains to see. Mariana that I was. Iemanja. Me!

Silvia, now I know. He gave you pills to sleep. How many did you take, my dear? Roderigo, watch out, they'll make you pay....

Speak dears. I'm closer to you now, wade in and we will meet.

Mel, son, what can I say? You understand more now.

Closer dears. I hear your joyous sound. Drums like thunderclaps! Your drumming warms my living saint's blood, sounds reach from here to beyond and bounce back.

Wade in. Your flower petals on the water form our path. Wonderful: you offer me exactly what I want. Simple things. Bright chips of mirror, beautiful ribbons for my hair, new perfume, combs. Thank you so much.

Now, see me: glorious Iemanja! My blue and yellow beads, crystal jewelry, blue-feathered crown, my blouse of Hong Kong silk. This beauty, all you need.

Waves rise, waves fall—our pain.

Now what's this I see? Among the white skirts. Redheaded: here she is. On her knees. Vanessa, the English, comes to me. Come!

Like the others, offering seashells and starfish. How she stares! Here I am, Vanessa—It's Mariana, Me.

They are all so close. Anxious for me. For me to hear their prayers. To help them! They wade out, so near.

Vanessa, I can hear you. That's what you want? To marry Alvaro, after all?

You pour me a cup of wine, thank you. But I cannot do that, Vanessa, dear, not now. Don't resist, the future will tell you another tale.

I see your friends, closing doors to you. Bring me your pain. Join our family, dear. We opened the door to another room. Come in. We'll nourish you.

My sons and daughters of the saints. Here I am. Arrived!

Your child will be Mel's daughter, Vanessa. I owe you my support, my generosity. Daughters of Iemanja in Brazil, me and you.

Vanessa, do you feel me, can you hear? You do? Marvelous! Look around you, to your brothers and sisters.

Now, be-decked gloriously with stars and shells I mount. Out of the sea, out of candlelight, out of the foam I rise. I come in and then I go out.

I leave. Take the medicine, dears. My only recipe: a dose of love so bitter, love so sweet, love so bittersweet.

—

—

About the author

Originally from New York City, Reid Baron lived in Brazil during the 1970's, working as a newspaper editor, translator and interpreter, and always writing. From 1980-2016, while living in Takoma Park, Maryland, he edited and published galleries magazine, *a guide to Washington/Baltimore metro area art galleries. For several years he also edited* The Takoma Park Newsletter.

With his wife Deborah Gay, a painter and printmaker, Reid has two children, Alexander and Oliver. The family home is now in West Virginia.

He has previously published "Shoot the Breeze," a basketball novel as a kindle e-book, and has a section of poems included in "The Music of the Aztecs," by the poets of the DC Magic Theater Poetry Club, at PonyOneDog Press.

Made in the USA
Middletown, DE
24 June 2023

32622341R00139